William Rhic Taggar

COMPANION READER VOLUME III
A TREASURY OF TEN SUMMERTIME CHILDREN'S STORIES

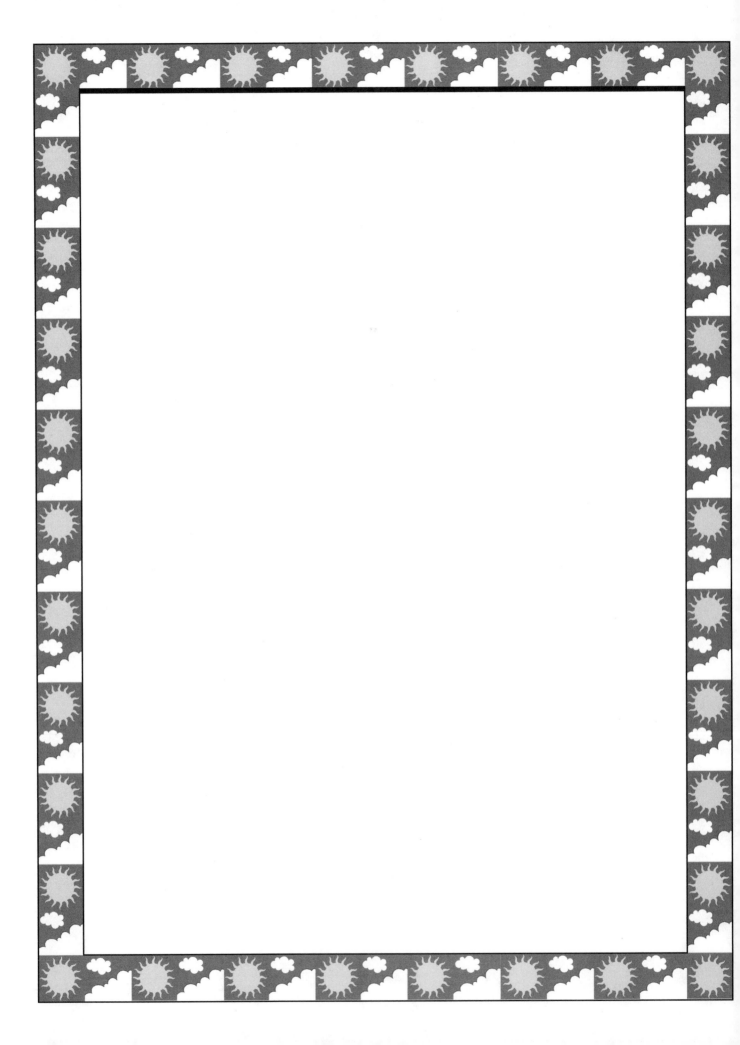

COMPANION READER VOLUME III

A TREASURY OF TEN SUMMERTIME CHILDREN'S STORIES

Stories by: **William R. McTaggart**

Illustrations by: **Eugene J. Hibbard**

SAN 299-8025

Published by *Gramma Books Publishing* Co.
Box 400
Oden, Michigan 49764
Web Site: www.grammabooks.com

Publisher's Cataloging-in-Publication
(*Provided by Quality Books, Inc.*)

McTaggart, William, R.
    Companion reader Volume III, A treasury of ten summertime children's stories / stories
by William R. McTaggart ; illustrations by Eugene J. Hibbard. -- 1st ed.
        p.   cm.
    Includes bibliographical references.
    ISBN: 0-9669285-1-2
    SUMMARY : Original values-oriented stories, including "The rooster who crowed too much"
and "A walk in the woods with Grandma.".

    1. Children's stories, American.   2. Animals -- Juvenile fiction.   I. Hibbard, Eugene J., ill.
II. Title.   III. Title : Treasury of ten summertime children's stories.

PZ7.M478836Co 1999   [Fic]
                    QBI99-24

Printed in the United States of America

10   9   8   7   6   5   4   3   2   1

A Gift of Love

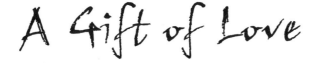

Read to a child at one and two,
fill young lives with love -- oh yes, yours too.

Read to children at three and four,
they're bound to ask for more and more.

Read tales to them at five, six and seven,
endow young minds with earthly heaven.

Read to kids at nine and ten -- listen too --
their weighty cares are all brand new.

Read to youth in their teens,
share favorite stories and fondest dreams.

Reading with children yields gifts to treasure.
Love of books -- no sweeter pleasure.

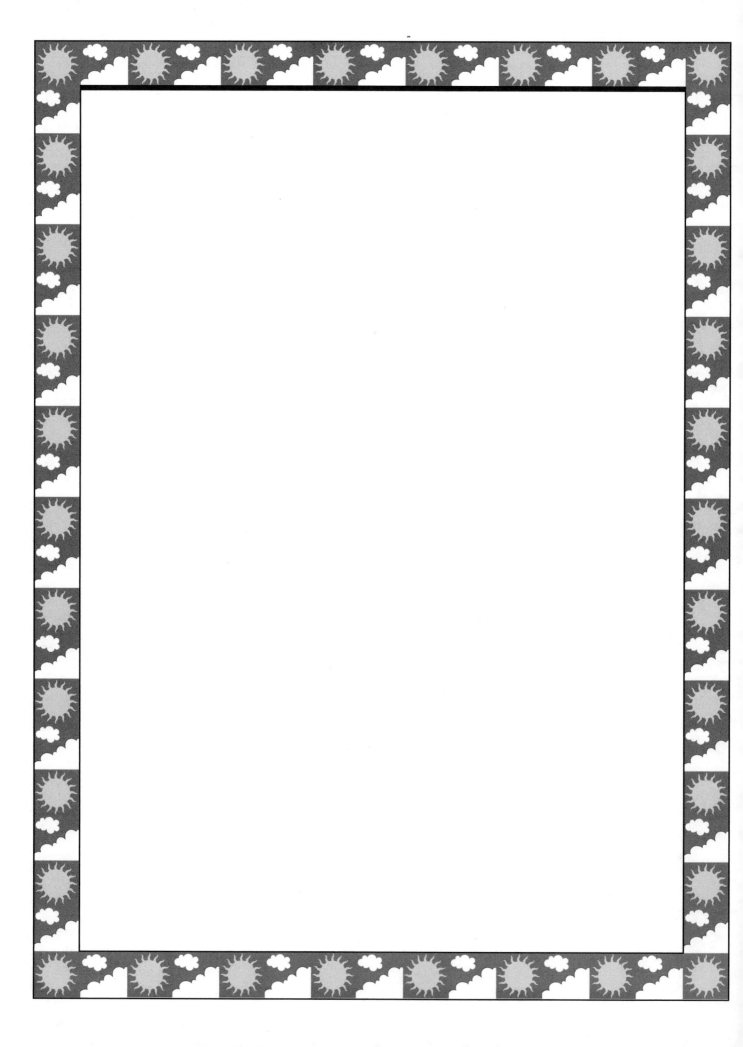

CONTENTS

POEMS

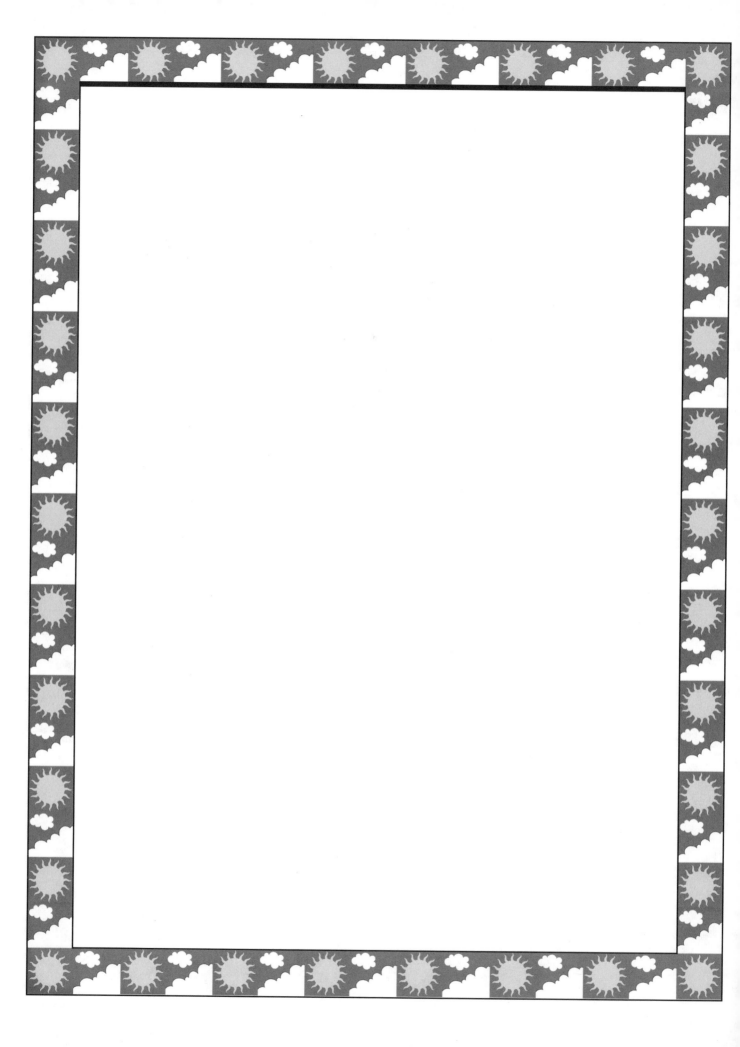

THE BOY WHO BECAME A FROG

Once upon a time, long ago, there was a very nice family who lived in a small village near a lake. Father worked at the mill all day to earn a living for the family. Mother tended the garden and managed their home. Mother was pretty and kind, and deeply loved father and their three children. John was the eldest child, Joseph was the middle, and Gerald was the youngest. John and Joseph did not treat Gerald as brothers should. Gerald often had to play by himself.

One sunny, warm day Mother said to the children, "Would you like to go to the lake, where we can have a picnic and you can all go swimming? We will come back home before your father returns from work. Then we will have supper."

The children were very excited. They all cried, "Oh, yes. Let's go to the lake." They ran to put on their bathing suits while mother made a nice picnic lunch of peanut butter and jelly sandwiches, some sweet pickles and orange pop.

The lake was down the road. Each of the children took turns carrying the picnic basket as they walked to the lake. As they got close to the lake, John and Joseph ran to the shore and jumped into the water, leaving Gerald behind, all by himself. Gerald did not like being left behind, but he was used to it.

John and Joseph were playing in the water when Gerald came along and sat down at the edge of the lake. He wished he could play with them, but he did not want his older brothers to know he didn't like being left out of things. As Gerald sat there, throwing small pebbles into the water, a very large fish swam up. It looked up through the water at Gerald. Gerald had never seen a fish that big before so he stopped throwing pebbles.

Big Fish began to talk. He had a deep, soft, velvety, voice. Big Fish said, "Hello, little boy. Do you like to swim?"

At first, Gerald was scared. He had never talked to a fish before. But the fish seemed friendly and anyway, Gerald was much larger than the fish. So Gerald answered, "Yes, I like to swim, but I don't swim as well as my two older brothers."

Big Fish said, "Oh, don't pay any attention to them. They don't care about you. I can make you able to swim much better than either of them -- if you are interested."

Gerald was very interested. He would do almost anything to be better at something than his two older brothers. He said, "Oh, yes, I would very much like to swim better than my brothers. Then maybe they would play with me."

Big Fish said, "I have magic powers. I can turn you into a frog, and then you will be the best swimmer of all."

Gerald was small, but he was not afraid any longer. He liked to try new things, so he said, "That sounds like a lot of fun, but can you turn me back into a boy when it is time to eat mother's picnic lunch?"

Big Fish smiled a funny kind of smile out of one side of his mouth, and his eyes narrowed. Gerald thought it was a most peculiar smile. "Sure . . . ," the fish said, in his soft, velvety voice. "I can turn you back into a boy any time I want. I have lots of magic powers."

Gerald was brave, but sometimes he didn't think of everything ahead of time. He decided it would be fun to be able to swim better than his brothers, so he stood up and walked right out into the lake, all the way up to his chin. Suddenly, before you could snap your fingers, Gerald was a frog with green spots and huge feet just right for swimming.

Big Fish was much larger than Gerald, now that Gerald was a frog. And Big Fish wore the strange smile that made Gerald nervous.

"See," said Big Fish, "I told you I had magic powers. How do you like being a frog?"

"Well," said Gerald, as he kicked his frog feet a couple of times and went racing through the water faster than he had ever been able to swim before, "it's kind of fun all right. But I think I had better go back to shore. My mother may be fixing the picnic. Would you mind turning me back into a boy? I think I have been a frog long enough."

Big Fish looked at Gerald and smiled his strange smile with narrowed eyes. This made Gerald more nervous than ever. Then the fish said, "Pretty soon, pretty soon. Why don't you just swim around a little more out here in the deep water, where I can see how good of a swimmer you are?"

Gerald did not know what to do. Big Fish seemed very friendly and yet Gerald felt uneasy. Just then Gerald felt a tug on his hand. He turned and saw another frog pulling on him.

"Quick, come with me behind this log at the bottom of the lake. Big Fish plans to eat you up as soon as he gets you in deep water."

Gerald decided he should listen to the frog. He quickly whirled around. With two kicks of his frog feet, Gerald hid in the mud at the bottom of the lake behind a log, along with the other frog. Gerald could see Big Fish above him, cruising along with a very mean and hungry look on his face.

"Where are you frog? Speak up so that I can find you."

Gerald did not say a word and Big Fish swam past.

After Big Fish had gone away the frog quietly said to Gerald, "That was a close call. Big Fish is not friendly at all. He just pretends to be friendly. Then, when he gets little boys to become frogs, he lures them into the deep water and eats them. No sir, he is not nice."

"What am I to do?" Gerald said. "My mother fixed a nice picnic lunch. I want to become a boy again and have a peanut butter and jelly sandwich with some orange pop."

"You'll just have to wait here until Big Fish is far away. Then you can come up and sit on a lily pad with me. We'll get some lunch there."

Gerald and his new friend sat scrunched down in the mud alongside the log at the bottom of the lake for a long time. Then Gerald heard some other voices. "All clear. All clear," the voices said.

Gerald's friend said, "Those are some of the other frogs in the lake. We all watch out for Big Fish. He is gone now. We can swim up to the top, climb up on a lily pad and get our lunch." Up they swam.

When Gerald reached the surface of the water, he took a deep breath of air and then climbed up on a large lily pad. His friend sat on a neighboring lily pad. When Gerald got up on the lily pad he could see his mother standing on the shore, calling his name.

"GERALD, GERALD," she called. Gerald could see she was very worried.

He tried to answer her, but when he tried to say, "HERE I AM" all that came out was "RIBBIT, RIBBIT" which is frog language. Gerald's mother did not understand frog language at all. Finally, as Gerald watched, his mother sadly turned away, packed up the picnic lunch and the whole family walked away. Gerald felt terrible, even worse than when his two brothers wouldn't play with him.

"I guess I won't get my peanut butter and jelly sandwich," Gerald said.

"Well, here," said Gerald's new friend, "have a nice green fly I just caught. They are awfully good." He handed Gerald a big fly with a green head.

"A fly!" Gerald exclaimed. "Yuch, I don't eat flies."

"Better learn how," Gerald's friend said, "that's what frogs eat, you know."

"I just want to go back home," Gerald said. "I'm tired of being a frog, even though you are very nice yourself." Gerald tried his best to smile at his friend, but it's not easy to smile when you are not happy, and Gerald was not happy at all.

Gerald sat on the lily pad for a while, trying to figure out how he was going to rejoin his family and become a boy again. He wished he hadn't listened to Big Fish. Listening to Big Fish was a disaster. Now Gerald was lonely and hungry, and his family had left and gone home to supper. A drop of water ran out of the corner of Gerald's eye, but Gerald bit his lip and was brave. He knew he had gotten himself into this mess and it was up to him to get himself out of it.

The main problem was how to become a boy again. Big Fish said he had the magic power to turn him back into a boy, but if Gerald went looking for Big Fish he would probably be eaten up. He certainly could not trust Big Fish, and frankly, he doubted that Big Fish would use his magic to help him. It was a serious problem all right.

Gerald turned to his new friend, who was happily catching flies on the end of his tongue. "Do you know how I can turn myself back into a boy?"

Gerald's friend had just swallowed a fly. He was smacking his lips. Frog lips are very big and the smacking sound was quite loud --- SMACK, SMACK, SMACK. When he was done smacking his lips, he said, "You can turn back into a boy, but first you have to find your mother. If your mother hugs you, then you will turn back into a boy. In the meantime you might as well have a fly. They are very good this time of year. Just wait until a fly buzzes close to your nose then very quickly stick out your tongue and catch him. It's easy once you get the hang of it."

Gerald did not know how in the world he would be able to find his mother --- and get a hug. But he was hungry, so he sat very still on the lily pad and pretty soon a big green fly began to buzz over his head. When the fly got close Gerald stuck out his tongue and snapped up the fly. Gerald swallowed the fly. He didn't like it. Peanut butter and jelly sandwiches taste much better. But Gerald was not a fussbudget. If frogs ate bugs then so would he. After all, Gerald was now a frog. 'Go along to get along', as they say. Gerald still didn't like flies, but what could he do?

Gerald sat on the lily pad wishing he hadn't listened to Big Fish. He was very lonely for his family, even for his two brothers who didn't treat him very well.

When Gerald's mother and two brothers got home they missed Gerald. Gerald's two brothers felt especially bad because they knew they hadn't been nice to their little brother. When Gerald's father came home from work he said, "Where is Gerald?"

Gerald's mother said, "I think he must have drowned at the lake. He went swimming and then we never saw him again. We called and called, but he never answered. All we could hear were frogs singing, 'Ribbit, Ribbit', but no Gerald. We finally gave up and came home."

Gerald's brothers knew what had happened and they sat silently looking very sad. Even though they hadn't treated Gerald like brothers should treat each other, they still liked him a lot. Now that Gerald wasn't with the family, they really missed him terribly.

John spoke up first, "I think he turned into a frog."

Then Joseph said, "Yes, the last time we saw Gerald he was sitting on the shore talking to a big fish. And then he went swimming alongside the fish. We heard the fish tell Gerald he could turn Gerald into a frog if he wanted. The next thing we saw was a frog swimming right where Gerald had been."

"Well," said the father, "it's been known to happen. The fish is not large enough to eat a little boy, but if he can talk a boy into letting himself be turned into a frog, then the fish makes a meal out of the frog. If that is what happened it is very bad for Gerald. We must go back to the lake and hope that when Gerald was turned into a frog he saw what the fish was up to and was fast enough and smart enough to get away without being eaten."

They all hurried back to the lake and began to call for Gerald.

Gerald heard them, but so did Big Fish. And Big Fish decided that if Gerald began to swim toward shore there might be a chance to catch him and eat him. Big Fish began cruising among the lily pads looking for Gerald.

Gerald could see his father on the shore of the lake. He was carrying a big club and peering into the water looking for Big Fish. But there was a good distance between where Gerald was sitting on the lily pad and the shore. If Gerald tried to swim to shore Big Fish surely would catch him. Gerald knew he would have to get closer to shore in order to lure Big Fish near to where his father was standing. It would be dangerous, but there was no other choice. And there was no time to lose.

First Gerald would have to fool Big Fish into thinking he was heading in a different direction. Wasting no time, Gerald jumped to a floating log toward the middle of the lake. He deliberately splashed the water with his left rear foot as he jumped. Big Fish heard the splash and began swimming toward the middle of the lake, eager to catch his dinner. Gerald could see Big Fish coming toward him. He splashed the water again to entice Big Fish closer. As Big Fish glided under the log where Gerald was sitting, Gerald quickly turned back toward shore. He swam and hopped from lily pad to lily pad until he was near his father. Then he reached into the water from his lily pad with his right foot and splashed the water again to attract Big Fish. By this time Big Fish was very angry. He knew he had been tricked. He turned toward the direction of the splash. Gerald jumped up and down on the lily pad, making sure Big Fish could see him. Then he splashed the water again.

Big Fish was plenty smart. That is how Big Fish got to be as big and old as he was. If he had kept his head, he would never have swum so close to shore, but he was furious. He could see Gerald on the lily pad jumping up and down, and that made him madder than ever. He was so angry he paid no attention to Gerald's father standing on the shore with his club.

Big Fish leaped out of the water, over the top of the lily pad, intending to snap up Gerald in one bite of his powerful jaws. But Gerald knew exactly what he was doing. He knew that Big Fish would be coming after him in a blind rage. He waited until Big Fish had jumped from the water and was in the air, unable to change direction. It would be close. At the last instant Gerald jumped sideways out of the way.

Gerald's father had seen the frog hopping from lily pad to lily pad taunting the fish, luring it to where he was standing on the shore. Father was ready. As Big Fish leaped from the water, Gerald's father swung the club and smacked Big Fish right on the head, killing him as dead as a mackerel.

Gerald's father hoped that the courageous frog was Gerald, but he didn't know for sure. If Big Fish had already swallowed Gerald they would have to get him out of Big Fish's stomach fast.

Gerald's father grabbed the dead fish and quickly took out his knife. Then he carefully cut open the belly of the fish. He had to be careful in case Gerald had already been swallowed and was in the fish's belly. The whole family crowded around. There were no frogs in the fish's belly and they breathed a sigh of relief.

They turned back to the lake and called to Gerald.

With Big Fish out of the way, Gerald quickly swam up to shore, hollering as loudly as he could, "RIBBIT, RIBBIT, RIBBIT," which in frog language means, "HUG ME, HUG ME, HUG ME." Even though Gerald's mother didn't exactly understand what Gerald was saying she picked up the frog, washed the mud from the frog's stomach, and hugged him ever so gently.

With that, the frog turned back into Gerald, and the whole family ran up and hugged him, especially his two brothers who felt partly responsible for Gerald's terrible predicament.

The brothers decided right then that they would include Gerald whenever they played together. They were very proud of Gerald for being so brave despite the great danger of being eaten alive. They were amazed at how clever Gerald had been to trick Big Fish and make his escape. The brothers decided they had a very smart younger brother.

The sun was going down and as dusk descended upon the lake one frog in the lake began to sing. Then another and another and another. Soon thousands of frogs were singing together in beautiful harmony, "*Ribbit*, **RIBBIT**, Ribbit, **RIBBIT** . . . ." Some voices were low and some were high but they all blended together in a wonderful chorus.

John and Joseph turned to their younger brother. Gerald was the only one in the family who understood frog language. "What are they saying, Gerald?"

Gerald said, "They are saying '**Thank you. Thank you. Thank you for getting rid of Big Fish**.' For the first time in many years the frogs can live in peace and without the fear of being eaten."

Then Gerald's two brothers asked, "What was it like being a frog, Gerald?"

And Gerald, who was delighted to be back with his family, replied, "Well, it was a scary adventure. I sure am not going to listen to any more big fish who try to talk me into things when I know better. And I still like peanut butter and jelly sandwiches a lot more than flies."

The End

TEA WITH THE QUEEN

One sunny day on the first day of May
When Susan was sitting
Just doing her knitting

Came a tap at the door.
Tap-a-tap, tap.
A quiet little rap.

23

Susan dropped her knitting
And leaped to her feet.
A visit with friends is ever so sweet.

When she opened the door
She was nearly struck dumb
For there was the Queen of the whole kingdom.

Susan bowed to the Queen.
"Won't you please come in?
Oh yes, your Highness, please come in."

"Thank you my dear," said the Queen most serene.
"I wish not to disturb your time of ease
But a brief moment, if you so please."

Susan replied with a curtsy
As nice as could be,
"May I honor my Queen with a cup of hot tea?"

"That would be charming," said the Queen with a smile.
"And may I ask of you,
Would you care to join me in a cup of tea too?"

"Oh yes, my Queen.
That would be my fondest pleasure
A delight to me of deepest measure."

So Susan scurried about
And poured them some tea.
"I do hope the tea is tasty, your majesty."

"I'm sure it will be perfect,
Susan, my dear.
Your manners are splendid, that much is clear."

As the Queen and Susan
Sat sipping their tea
Susan said, "In what small way may I be of service to
thee?"

"I come to ask for your help,"
Said the Queen. "You see,
A visit with you seemed most fitting to me.

"For a lady so young,
I hear you are wise, as well as quite nice.
Which brings me to come, seeking advice.

"We search for a name to announce to our people
To celebrate the joy of this bright spring day
This very first day of the month of May."

"You ask what I fancy?" said Susan in awe.
"A name for the day when May begins?
The day of the year of our happiest grins.

"How kind of you, your Majesty.
A great honor you bestow on me
Though I can only speak of the beauty I see.

"To me this day is nature's finest gift
As exquisitely woven as pure Irish lace
A caress of sunshine upon winter's pale face.

"I visit our garden to gaze at the flowers.
The lush of the meadow offers soft tender seat,
Where I kick off my shoes and wiggle my feet.

"The first day of May," said Susan with feeling,
"Is my own beginning of spring
And spring, you know, is a most glorious thing.

"The grass is so green.
The air is so fresh.
All the flowers are dressed in their very best dress.

"We are proper on Sunday.
And pleasant on Monday.
But the first day of May is my very own ---- Funday!

"That's what I call the first day of May
Announcing the start of summer's gay ball
The very best day of all of them all."

"Well, thank you my dear.
I believe you have answered my quest
Your name for the day is surely the best.

"I shall return to the palace and tell it to Alice,"
Said the Queen as she rose
To give fair Susan a pretty red rose.

Then saying good-bye
The Queen rode to the palace
There to confer with her kind cousin, Alice.

From that day forward the first day of May
The Queen proclaimed
Shall always be Funday, the day's special name.

And every year since, on the first day of May
With blossoms of spring in their most wondrous dress
Susan's Funday is the name chosen best.

A truth Kings and Queens of all nations
May wisely recall
Children often know the best names of all.

The End

Nothin' To Do

Jake and Joe
Were seven and eight.
Free for the summer
When they had opened the gate

Of school in the spring
To let the kids out
With nothin' to do
'Cept wander about.

Time on their hands
Bored don't you see.
Joe said to his mother
As nice as could be,

"Please Mother dear
can we go to the lake?
To fish and to play
Just you, me and Jake?"

So off they all went
To swim in the lake.
Lie in the sun
Where they would bake.

And when they got tired
Of sittin' around
No TV to watch
No pals to be found

They'd make up some fun
For their very own pleasure.
Explore the desert island.
Search for pirate treasure.

First they found a wooden box
To put some of their things --
Four marbles, three keys
And two Cracker Jack rings.

They whittled a sword
With a loop for their belt
In case they found trouble
With which must be dealt.

Climb into the boat
Swords at their side.
Sail to the island
With their treasure to hide.

At the top of the island
they found a big tree.
Made a mark on their map
No pirates could see.

Then ten paces north
And six paces west
They found a secret place
To hide their treasure chest.

They dug a deep hole
Ten inches deep and twelve inches wide.
No pirates would find it
No matter how hard they tried.

Cover the box with dirt,
Leaves and some twigs.
Drag a big branch
To cover the digs.

Then folding the chart
All carefully marked
They crept back to the boat
Where they had parked.

Row back to the cottage
And after their nap
They'd remember the treasure
Unfold the secret map.

Sail to the island
With a great deal of pleasure.
They began the search
For the deep buried treasure.

"Quiet!" they said.
"Talk is forbidden.
The map will show us
Where the treasure is hidden."

Follow the trail,
To discover the end.
Make sure no pirates are hidin'
Round by the bend.

They found the big tree
Shown by a dot.
Ten paces north, six paces west,
'X' marks the spot.

Scrape off the leaves, signs of fresh dirt.
Could be hidden gold
Buried deep in the earth
By pirates of old.

Then they discovered the chest
With valuable things.
Four marbles, three keys
And two Cracker Jack rings.

They raised their fine swords and sang a sea ditty.
"Two brave men with their treasure chest
Of all the fierce pirates
We two are the best."

Back to the boat
With treasure in hand
They rowed their way home.
Best men in the land.

About that time
Father came home
From the city where he worked
All day to the bone.

"Hi, boys,
What have you been doing all day?
Keep yourselves busy
Out of Mom's way?"

With nothin' to do what could they say?
Sailed to the island and dug up some gold.
Like the fierce pirates
In days of the bold.

And tomorrow ---
They may build a stone castle
Capture a mean dragon
Or with a lion rassle ---

IF THERE'S NOTHIN' TO DO

The End

BETTER GET A NOSE --- QUICK!

Every spring when the winter snow melts, the pond behind Tommy Terwilliger's house fills to overflowing with fresh, clean water. The pond is shallow and the bright sun quickly warms the cold water which fills the pond. Tall grasses and weeds grow in the pond, and the pond is far enough from everything so that no one bothers it. It is a perfect place to raise baby frogs --- and every year mother frogs come from long distances to lay their eggs in the water among the weeds and grasses.

There is only one thing wrong with the pond. It drys up in the summer. To survive, the baby frogs have to learn to breathe out of the water before the pond drys up. The baby frogs do not know the pond is going to dry up. After the eggs are laid there is no one around to tell them what is going to happen when summer comes.

Now this may be hard to believe, but the truth is, once a mother frog has laid her eggs, she just up and leaves. She doesn't even hang around long enough for the eggs to hatch or to warn the baby frogs about the pond drying up. Maybe that's because baby frogs are smarter than people and they don't need their parents to take care of them. Anyway, that's the way it is with frogs.

Freddie started out as a frog egg in Tommy Terwilliger's pond. After Freddie hatched, he became a tiny tadpole. A tadpole is a very young frog, before it has grown legs or developed a nose. Sometimes people call tadpoles *polywogs*. Polywogs and tadpoles are the same. We'll call them tadpoles, but if you wish, you may call them polywogs. Polywog is kind of a fun word.

When Freddie was a young tadpole he had a long tail and gills for breathing like a fish. Tadpoles and fish need water to breathe.

Freddie was a cheerful tadpole and he was friends with many of the other tadpoles. They played together all day long without any responsibilities. They took naps whenever they wanted and sometimes, with nobody to tell them what they must do, they didn't take a nap at all. They didn't have to take out the garbage, because there wasn't any garbage.

And they didn't have to help dry the dishes, because they didn't have any dishes. It was a fun time.

But then, one day, without any warning, Freddie began to grow legs. He still had a tail, but tiny legs began to grow on his body, just like arms and legs on people. It was all part of nature's plan to start Freddie on his way to becoming a full-size frog. But it was strange, and Freddie didn't know what to make of it.

One of the other tadpoles in the pond swam up to Freddie and said, "Freddie, what are those funny things growing out of your body?"

"I think they may be legs," Freddie said. "They just started growing all by themselves."

"Do they hurt?" the other tadpole asked.

"No, they don't hurt. But they get in the way of my swimming. I used to be nice and round and streamlined. Now, with legs sticking out of my body, I can't swim as fast as before."

The other tadpole said, "Well, I don't want any legs growing on me. I would rather stay the way I am."

When the other tadpoles in the pond saw what was happening to Freddie many of them decided they didn't want to grow any legs either. They decided they wanted to remain tadpoles.

Some of the tadpoles, who weren't very nice, had a good time poking fun at Freddie. They would say mean things like, "Hey Freddie, those sure are funny looking legs. Where are your shoes?"

Or, "Wow, Freddie, you sure are a slow swimmer. We can beat the pants off all you guys with legs." Of course that was silly. Tadpoles don't have shoes or pants. Even the ones with legs don't have pants.

Sometimes the tadpoles who had decided not to grow legs would gather in a little group by themselves whispering to each other and giggling when they thought Freddie wasn't looking. They would point at Freddie and laugh, "Ha, ha, ha." Since they were under water it sounded more like, "Hurgle, hurgle, hurgle." No matter how it sounded, Freddie didn't think it was funny. It isn't much fun being laughed at.

Then, as if things weren't already bad enough, Freddie began growing a nose. It looked even more peculiar than his legs. The tadpoles laughed harder than ever and that made Freddie feel worse than before. They called Freddie "Old Big Nose." It's not a joke to be laughed at and called names just because you look different.

Sometimes Freddie would try to hide his legs from the others by holding them tight against his body. It was no use. He couldn't hide his nose and the other tadpoles kept right on laughing and making fun of him.

His legs grew longer and his nose grew bigger. It wasn't long before Freddie even started growing hands and feet.

Of course Freddie's brain was getting bigger and smarter too. Freddie had always had a pretty good brain. He was curious about everything and the smarter he got the more curious he became. He couldn't help himself. He wanted to see what was going on in other places in the pond, besides the small part of the pond where he was born. The tadpoles without legs were content to swim around in the same old places all day long, just playing around and poking fun at Freddie.

When Freddie tried to get the other tadpoles to come along with him to investigate other parts of the pond, they laughed at him and called him "Old Big Nose Smarty Pants". Actually they were afraid to venture very far from where they were born. They didn't care whether they learned anything new or not. They weren't very smart.

Freddie thought about pretending he was dumb, so that the tadpoles would like him and play with him more. But he soon found that was a waste of time. The others just wanted to hang around without doing much of anything. Finally Freddie decided if the others weren't interested he would explore by himself.

First he explored every corner of the pond. Then he decided to poke his head above the water to look around outside. Until that moment Freddie had always breathed through his gills under water. That was the only way he could breathe, because when he was a small tadpole, like the others, he didn't have a nose.

When Freddie poked his head above the water and took his first breath through his nose he was delighted by the sweet smell of fresh air. He filled his lungs and smelled the delicious fragrance of flowers growing along the shore of the pond.

He took another deep breath and suddenly realized he was breathing through his nose. What an exciting discovery! If he could breathe pure air outside the water in the pond, he no longer needed to stay in the water. He was free to explore the world!

It was an entirely different world above the water. The flowers at the edge of the pond were beautiful. The sunshine was so brilliant it made his eyes blink. He had never seen anything like this under water. It was a magnificent experience.

Freddie climbed out of the water to sit on a log that floated in the pond. The tadpoles in the pond looked up through the water and saw Freddie.

They called out, "What are you doing up there Freddie? You are supposed to stay down here in the pond, with us."

Freddie looked down at the tadpoles who had decided they didn't want to grow legs or a nose or to go exploring. He said, "Why this is a wonderful new world up here. You should come up and look around. There are trees and flowers and delicious smells of all kinds of things. You don't know what you are missing."

The tadpoles looked up and said, "We can't climb up on the log. We don't have your funny looking legs. We can't smell anything. We don't have your homely nose. We are quite content just the way we are."

"Well, that's too bad," Freddie said. "You better start growing some legs and noses so you can see what is going on in the rest of the world."

But the other tadpoles only laughed and said, "We like it here just fine. We get to play all day, take naps whenever we feel like it and nobody tells us what to do." Then they swam away.

Freddie was so excited he couldn't wait to explore. He hopped off the log, swam to the edge of the pond and climbed onto the shore. There he saw trees so high they reached right up into the sky. He saw birds with yellow noses and blue wings. He saw fleecy white clouds in the sky and gorgeous flowers. There were all kinds of wonderful things.

As he hopped along he came upon a fuzzy green caterpillar and decided to taste it. He stuck out his tongue, wrapped it around the caterpillar and flipped it right into his mouth, swallowing it whole. It was delicious and filled him right up. All the time he had been a tadpole back in the pond he had never tasted anything so good or as filling as the fuzzy green caterpillar. He decided one caterpillar a day was about all anybody could eat. When he had been a tadpole he had to keep eating all day long because the food in the pond was so tiny. Now he would have time for other things besides eating.

Soon he came to a woods. With a full stomach he was quite sleepy. He decided to rest a while and maybe take a nap. He crawled under some leaves beneath a tree and pulled the leaves up to his chin. When he awoke it was night time. Freddie looked up into the sky and saw the moon and bright stars filling the heavens. It was a magnificent sight. He stretched out with his hands behind his head to look up at the stars.

As he lay there, soaking up the peace and quiet of the forest, he heard singing from the other side of the woods. The voices blended together in a beautiful chorus. He thought to himself: "When it gets light I must find where that beautiful music is coming from."

When the sun came up Freddie set out in the direction of the singing he had heard during the night. Soon he came to a big lake. It was a grand lake, with sparkling blue water in the middle and lily pads, cattails and bull rushes along the shore. He could see many full grown frogs sitting on the lily pads. They had legs and noses, just like Freddie. He wondered if he might have hopped into frog heaven.

"Hi," Freddie called out to one of the frogs on a lily pad close to shore. "I'm having an adventure. I am looking for the singers I heard during the night."

"Hi, to you too," said the frog. "That was us. We frogs like to sing every night during the summer when the moon comes out. Do you sing? We need a good tenor."

"I don't know whether I can sing or not," Freddie said. "I never tried. I just became a frog a short time ago. I used to be a tadpole."

"Did you come from the pond on the other side of the woods?" asked the frog.

"Well, yes I did," Freddie replied. "How did you know?"

"That is where most of us were born," the friendly frog in the lake said. "After we grew legs and a nose we went exploring, just like you are doing now. We discovered this lake. And it's a good thing we did too, because the pond dries up in the summer. This lake never dries up. It's a wonderful place to live. You are welcome to stay if you wish. You will like it here."

"You say the pond drys up in the summer?" Freddie said, quite concerned.

"Oh, yes. Along about the middle of July the hot summer sunshine evaporates all the water in the shallow pond. It just drys up."

"What about the tadpoles who are still in the pond?!" Freddie exclaimed. "They don't have noses. They need water to live. What happens to them?"

"I'd rather not say," the frog replied. "It is not a pleasant thought."

Freddie knew there was not a moment to be lost. He must hurry back to the pond to warn the tadpoles. The sun was getting higher in the sky every day, and the days were becoming longer and warmer. July was less than a month away.

Freddie wheeled around, waved good-bye to the friendly frog on the lily pad and began hopping back toward the pond as fast as he could. It was nearly nightfall by the time he reached the pond.

He jumped into the water, calling out to all the tadpoles, "Come quick -- come quick. I have very important news."

Even though the tadpoles had made fun of Freddie while he was growing legs and a nose, they still liked him. Freddie had always been pleasant to them, even when they said mean things to him. The tadpoles gathered around. First he told them about all the wondrous things he had seen up

on the land. He told them of the great high trees and the beautiful clouds in the sky. He told them about colorful birds and marvelous flowers. He told them how good juicy caterpillars tasted. He told them about the other frogs that sang in the night and of the magnificent lake with cattails, bull rushes and water lilies where you can sit in the sun and take naps.

The tadpoles were fascinated by Freddie's exciting adventure. A few of the smartest tadpoles decided they too would like to start growing legs and noses so they could climb out of the pond and explore the wonderful world above.

But some of the tadpoles pooh-poohed the whole idea. They were perfectly happy to keep right on being tadpoles, so that they could play all day without a worry in the world. They started to swim away.

Freddie called after them, "But wait, I haven't told you the most important part."

The tadpoles stopped to listen.

"This whole pond will begin to dry up soon. As the weather becomes warmer and warmer the water will become shallower and shallower, until finally, by the middle of July there will be no water at all."

"Oh come on now Freddie," one of the tadpoles said. It was the same tadpole who had laughed the hardest at Freddie's new legs and nose. "You're just trying to scare us. We have plenty of water. It's nice and warm and we have more food than we've ever had. You paint a pretty picture of the outside world, but we know there are many dangers up there. We could get eaten by a big bird or a snake. Snakes like to eat frogs, we've heard. It's too risky." He turned to some of his fellow tadpoles. "We like it right here, don't we fellows?"

A few of the tadpoles who were his buddies gathered around him. "Yeah, Freddie, you're just trying to scare us. We like it fine right here. Why don't you go back where you came from?" Then they laughed and swam away.

But a good number of the tadpoles hung back. "Is it true Freddie? Is the pond really going to dry up?"

"Yes," Freddie said. "It is true. There is no time to lose. If you start right now and work as hard as you can to grow legs and noses you may just make it out before the pond drys up. The frogs who live on the lake have seen the pond dry up every summer.

"Don't take my word for it. Think for yourselves. You can already feel the water get warmer each day as the sun gets higher in the sky. Some of the water in the pond is evaporating every day. It is already shallower, just in the two days I was away."

The tadpoles who had stayed behind to listen to what Freddie told them clustered together. "It's true all right," one of them said to the others. "The sun is getting hotter every day and the pond is getting shallower."

"But won't the snow melt and fill the pond back up?" one of the listeners asked.

"There isn't going to be any more snow until next winter. That is many months from now. Freddie knows and he is telling us the truth. The pond will be completely dry in less than a month. If we have not grown noses by then we'll be goners. I'm going to warn the others one more time. It's up to them. They can decide for themselves whether they want to grow up."

Those who listened to Freddie and thought things out for themselves were the lucky ones. By mid-July their noses and legs were big enough to let them climb out from the last bit of water in the pond, barely in the nick of time.

The remaining tadpoles, who had chosen not to grow up, would never be able to see the wonders of the outside world. They had simply played around a little too long.

The End

THE FORGETFUL SQUIRREL

Once upon a time there was a young squirrel who forgot things. Edward didn't forget things on purpose and he didn't forget everything. He never forgot dinnertime. He never forgot to go outside and play on Saturday when there was no school. He just forgot some things.

Sometimes he forgot to say 'thank you' when his mother made breakfast for him. Sometimes he forgot to say 'please' when he wanted an extra piece of toast. There were a few times he even forgot to do his homework and then he would get bawled out by his teacher. That wasn't fun at all. Edward did the best he could -- he just didn't have a very good memory.

During the week Edward and his brothers and sisters went to squirrel school. There they learned how to jump from tree to tree without falling. They learned how to walk on a telephone line high above the street, so they wouldn't have to cross the street on the ground and maybe get run over by a truck. At school they learned how to flick their tails and chatter when they became excited or to warn other squirrels when danger was near. Most important, squirrels had to learn how to find acorns when the oak trees dropped them on the ground at the end of summer.

Squirrels also have to learn how to bury acorns in the ground, so that when winter comes and food is hard to find they can retrieve the acorns for supper. That was the problem. Edward learned how to bury the acorns, but after he had hidden them he couldn't remember where he had put them.

When the acorns began to fall off the oak trees, Edward and his brothers and sisters would gather them, as they had been instructed to do in school. When they found two acorns they tucked one acorn in each side of their cheeks, and then they searched for a place to hide them.

Edward wanted to be able to please his mother when she needed acorns for dinner during the long winter. He did not want anyone to steal his acorns, so he scampered off

through the woods to a secret place. Then he buried them. Edward buried more acorns than any of his brothers and sisters. He was very proud of himself.

One day when winter came and the snow got deep Edward's mother said to him, "Edward, dear, it will be time for supper soon. I believe we will have stewed acorns for dinner tonight. Would you please get me two acorns for dinner?"

Edward was very pleased that his mother had asked him to fetch his acorns. He liked it when his mother treated him like a grownup even though he was only a year old. (A squirrel who is a year old is the same age as a person who is seven years old.)

Edward scampered down the tree in which his family lived and started to search for the acorns he had hidden in the fall. First he dug through the snow at the foot of the tree. He didn't find any acorns there. The tree was a maple tree and acorns only grew on oak trees. Then he ran over to the big tree next door. It was a basswood tree. He dug through the snow and once again could not find any acorns. Edward had forgotten that acorns do not grow on basswood trees either.

Finally, he sat down to think. When you have a problem it is always better to think before you start running all over the place. Edward remembered he had carried the acorns through the woods to a secret place where only he would be able to find them. That was the problem. Because of his poor memory, Edward couldn't remember where his secret hiding place was located. He thought and he thought, but no matter how hard he thought, he couldn't remember.

By now it was getting close to the time when his mother would need to start cooking the acorns. She planned on cooking the acorns in a pot with some carrots and celery to make a nice acorn stew. It would take an hour of cooking before the acorns would be good and tender. Edward had never been one to wander off and his mother began to get worried. She poked her head out of the hole in the tree and called to Edward. But he could not hear her. He was running around in the woods, frantically looking for his secret acorn hiding place.

Edward's mother called Samuel, Edward's older brother, who was two years old.

"Samuel," she said, "I sent Edward out over an hour ago to find two acorns for dinner. He should have been back by now but he hasn't returned. I am getting worried. Would you please go out and see if you can find him? Maybe he got lost in the woods."

Everybody in the family liked Edward because he was a happy squirrel and fun to be around, even if at times he was absent-minded. They knew he had a poor memory, but they didn't hold it against him. All of us have something we are not so good at.

Samuel ran down the tree and began searching for his younger brother. First he looked under the tree where the family lived. He could see someone had been digging in the snow beneath the tree and also by the basswood tree next door. Samuel didn't find Edward there, so he ran into the forest looking for him, calling as he went. Edward had left a trail of freshly dug holes where he had searched for his acorns. It was easy to follow the trail of leaves that had been scattered on top of the snow.

Finally, deep in the forest, Samuel found his brother. "What in the world are you doing, Edward?" Samuel asked. "Mother wants you to bring two acorns home for supper. I followed your trail through the forest. There aren't any acorns here. These are all maple trees, birch trees and basswood trees. Don't you remember what they taught us in school? Only oak trees have acorns."

"I know that," Edward replied, almost in tears. "I'm looking for the secret place where I buried the acorns last fall. I hid a lot of acorns because I wanted to please Mother when she sent me out to find acorns in the winter for supper.

"But now I cannot remember where I hid them. I have been thinking and thinking, but I cannot remember. I so wanted to please Mother. I don't know what to do. I haven't been able to find a single acorn and my paws are all cut and hurt from digging through the snow and frozen ground."

Edward sat down in the snow and buried his face in his hands. He felt terrible because he had failed.

Samuel sat down beside Edward and put his arm around his brother. "That's okay, Edward," he said. "We all forget things once in a while. I remember once I buried a dozen beechnuts and then couldn't find a single one. Mother had promised all of us beechnut pie for supper that night. I felt terrible too, but those things happen. Maybe you will remember where you hid the acorns later.

"Anyway," Samuel continued. "I know where there is a big oak tree. We'll be able to find a couple of acorns there. Come with me. We'll dig them up and take them home to Mother."

"Oh, can we?" Edward exclaimed. "Can we pretend I found them and maybe Mother won't be mad at me for forgetting?"

"I'm afraid we can't do that," Samuel said. "We must always be honest. It is much worse being dishonest than admitting we make mistakes sometimes. I'm sure Mother will understand. It would be best to tell her what really happened."

The two brothers ran through the woods to a big oak tree where many acorns had fallen before the snow came. They both dug and dug and soon each of them had found an acorn hidden under the snow. They tucked the acorns in their cheeks and ran back home through the forest. They could see their mother peeking out of the hole in the tree looking for them. She had a worried look on her face.

"Here we are, Mother," Samuel said, "Edward is all right."

"Where in the world have you been, Edward? I have been very worried," Edward's mother said.

Edward looked toward his older brother, hoping Samuel would tell his mother that Edward could not remember where he had hidden the acorns he buried last fall. Samuel said nothing. He waited for his younger brother to tell his mother the truth.

Finally, Edward said, "I am sorry, Mother. I couldn't remember where I had hidden my acorns. I so wanted to make you proud of me by bringing acorns home when the snow got deep. I hid the acorns in a secret place in the forest. But when you asked me to bring some acorns for the stew, I just couldn't remember. I dug all over in the woods, but I couldn't find them. I am so ashamed of myself." Edward hung his head.

"It's all right, Edward." His mother smiled, putting her arm around her son. "I am real proud that you did your very best. That's what counts. None of us is perfect. You will probably remember in time. Let me bandage your sore paws. I can see you hurt them digging through the snow."

Mother served the acorn stew for supper, but Edward wasn't very hungry. He kept trying to remember where he had buried his acorns. For the life of himself he could not remember. It looked like they would be lost forever. Even though his brothers and sisters were kind and would not tease him about his memory, Edward was embarrassed.

All the other squirrels had good memories. Edward knew he was different from them, and that made him feel bad. He could try to pretend it didn't matter -- but to Edward it mattered a lot. When you are young nobody likes to be different. Edward wondered if he would ever feel good about himself.

It was not a fun winter for Edward. From time to time, when the snow was not too deep, he would go into the forest by himself searching for the acorns. He dug here and he dug there, but he never found his secret hiding place. He had hidden the acorns too well.

Finally, when spring came and the days began to get warmer and warmer the whole family decided to go on a picnic. Mother made up a picnic basket of hazelnuts and beechnuts for snacks and acorn sandwiches for the main meal.

They walked a long distance, until they came to a sunny knoll in the forest surrounded by tall trees. The children ran up the trees, jumping from one to the other, as Mother spread the picnic tablecloth on the grass below.

Everyone in the family was running and jumping here and there, having a wonderful time romping in the woods and chasing each other up the trees. Suddenly, Samuel called from high in a tree, "Look, look! I think I see where Edward buried his acorns last fall."

The family stopped what they were doing and looked up at Samuel who was sitting on a limb high in the tree. He was pointing to a place on the ground below. The family scampered to where Samuel was pointing. There, in at least

two dozen places, were tiny green acorn sprouts poking their heads through the leaves on the forest floor. The acorns had been planted in exactly the right place and at exactly the right depth in the ground to begin growing new oak trees.

It would take many years before the young trees produced acorns, but a start had been made. All because Edward had forgotten where he had hidden the acorns. Had he remembered, the acorns would have been dug up and eaten by now.

Edward's mother and his brothers and sisters gathered around Edward. His mother hugged Edward and said, "See, children. Each of us has a special talent. Some of us have good memories and are able to hide our winter food and then bring the acorns home when we need them. That is very important. But other talents are just as important.

"Your brother Edward may have a poor memory, but he is a wonderful tree farmer. He planted his acorns in this sunny clearing in the forest at just the right depth below the leaves. They will grow into giant oak trees and provide food for squirrels for many years in the future. He may be the best tree farmer in the whole forest. We are very proud of you, Edward."

Edward still couldn't remember very well, but he was proud of being the best tree farmer in the forest. That was important too. He was no different than he had been before the family discovered his tiny new acorn seedlings, but for the first time in his life he felt good all over.

The End

THE GRAY BANDANNA

"This year we are going to award YMCA bandannas to the twelve best campers. We will announce the winners at the end of the two-week session," announced Mr. Crampton, the camp director. He held up a beautiful gray bandanna. He folded it into a triangular shape and draped it around his neck and over his shoulders for all the campers to see and admire.

"Each of you may want to make a leather kerchief band at the craft shop, just in case you are the winner of one of the bandannas," he continued. Mr. Crampton held up a colorfully decorated kerchief band. A kerchief band is a leather strip tied together at each end to form a small circle. The corners of the bandanna are pulled through the band to hold the bandanna in place around your neck.

The camp director continued, "I will leave the bandanna on the table so that everyone can look it over. Any one of you can be a winner. Age does not matter. We will announce the winners at the evening powwow next Friday night, the last day of this session. Good luck to all of you."

With our session half over, I knew Pete Waldron would be one of the winners. He was the best hitter on the camp baseball team. Walter Spencer would be another winner. He was the best swimmer in camp. And there were plenty of others who would qualify as one of the twelve best campers. I was not one of them. But, what the heck? I was having a good time at the YMCA camp on Crystal Lake anyway.

The campers crowded around the table to get a better look at the bandanna. It was a beautiful blue-gray color. In one corner in red stitching were the words, YMCA - Crystal Lake Camp. A guy would be plenty proud to wear one of those bandannas.

There were 150 boys in camp. Our ages ranged from seven to about fifteen. The older boys were the best bowmen, the best swimmers, the best baseball players, the best everything. I was only ten, a pretty good competitor in my own age group, but no match for the big guys. The camp director said the age of the winners did not matter. We all had a chance to be a winner.

I thought to myself, Who cares anyway? But secretly, I did care. I sure would like to win one of those bandannas, although I knew there was not the slightest chance. Still -- maybe it would be a good idea to make a kerchief band at craft shop -- just in case.

A piece of leather cost twenty-five cents at the craft shop. The following week many of the campers were busy making leather bands to slide over the ends of a bandanna, just like the old-time cowboys. When cowboys were out on the trail, bandannas were mighty handy for keeping dust off of their faces and for wiping sweat from their brows on hot days roundin' up stray dogies. Dogies are what they call young cattle. We didn't have any cattle at 'Y' camp, but it's good to be prepared.

A bandanna can also be turned around and used to cover your face, like the old-time bank robbers. But most of us had no reason to hide our identity, except maybe in fun.

To make a kerchief band we first cut a piece of leather four inches long and one inch wide. Then we used a hole punch to punch holes at each end of the leather strip. The holes were for colored laces to tie the leather into a circular band after it had been decorated. We soaked the leather in water overnight to make it soft. The next day we used marking tools to emboss the pliant leather. We could put Indian symbols on the leather or stamp the words: YMCA - Crystal Lake Camp -- along with our initials. When the leather dried, we painted the embossed markings with bright fingernail polish to decorate the design.

Most of us knew we wouldn't win one of the twelve bandannas, but the kerchief bands can be used with any bandanna or to hold one of our fathers' large handkerchiefs draped around our necks. It was a good idea to have a bandanna, even if it wasn't one of the coveted Best Camper bandannas with the words, "YMCA - Crystal Lake Camp", embroidered in red at the corner.

Friday night arrived. The campers assembled for the Powwow. We always had a few skits put on by the campers, but the bandanna award presentation was what we were all waiting for. It was no surprise. Most of the winners were the boys who pitched winning softball games, won the races or created the best craft shop projects. There were a few younger campers who won an award. They seemed to be the ones who had fun and laughed a lot. I had a lot of fun at camp, but I was not one of the winners.

I hadn't really expected to win, but I had my kerchief band in my pocket, just in case. Might as well admit it. I was disappointed. Maybe next year .....

☼ ☼ ☼ ☼ ☼ ☼ ☼ ☼ ☼ ☼ ☼ ☼

When next summer finally arrived I was determined to win one of the twelve bandannas -- at any cost. As part of my personal *winning* campaign I was the first to grab the broom and sweep out the cabin each day. I raked the swimming beach, even if I wasn't asked, and sometimes when it did not need raking. I followed the counselors wherever they went, eager to do their bidding, trying to make points. Frankly, I was a pain in the neck.

In other years I had been an eager participant in all the camp fun. This year was different. I was on a mission and I did not have fun. In fact, I had a miserable time the entire two weeks of camp -- but I was confident I would surely be one of the twelve winners who were announced at the pow-wow on the last night of camp.

The big night finally came. I made sure I was at the lodge ten minutes early to grab a front seat in the assembly hall. I wanted to be ready to receive one of the twelve Best Camper awards -- a beautiful gray bandanna with the words "YMCA - Crystal Lake Camp" splendidly embroidered in red on one corner.

Somehow, in addition to all the self-imposed chores, I had found time to make a beautiful new leather kerchief band. It was colorfully decorated with Indian signs and a tomahawk stamped into the leather. The new band was in my pocket. From time to time during the Powwow I put my hand into the pocket to make sure the band was there, ready to secure the award around my neck when it was presented to me.

Only twelve of the 150 campers could receive an award. That was an honor of which my parents would be proud. I had not told them about the award, but they would find out when they picked me up at the end of the session on Saturday morning. Then I could tell them the whole story.

The camp director stepped up on the stage of the Camp Lodge. The bandannas were carefully laid out on a table next to him.

"Well, men," he began. "Now is the time to reveal the names of the twelve best campers of the session. Many of you have been very good campers and no doubt many more of you should be among the winners. But we only have twelve bandannas to give out. Those of you who are lucky enough to win a bandanna can know that the counselors and the rest of the camp staff voted on who would be among the twelve winners. The winners are ..."

He paused, reaching into his pocket for a paper that contained the names of the winners. My name would probably be at the top of the list. I had certainly worked hard enough to make sure I earned it.

The camp director began reading. One by one the winners were asked to step forward and stand before the assembled campers. Finally there were twelve winners standing in front of the assembly. I was not one of them. I could not believe it! I had wasted the entire two weeks working my head off, cleaning the cabin, raking the beach, and picking up after the counselors. Sure, I could understand why the winners were chosen. Mostly they were the leaders in various sports or they had accomplished some other outstanding achievement. But not one of them had worked as hard as I had. Not one of them had wasted the entire session trying to be "Mr. Goody-Goody Two Shoes" -- the best camper ever.

The ceremony ended. I bit my tongue and kept my feelings to myself as I walked to the front of the assembly hall to congratulate the twelve winners. No one would ever know how I felt deep down. Truthfully, I felt terrible.

Well let me tell you, next year would be different. I would raise the dickens and have a good time. I'd do my share of camp chores all right, but let somebody else spend their time cleaning the john, and fawning after the counselors. Never again would I throw away the best two weeks of my summer chasing after a silly award while everybody else was having a great time.

❂ ❂ ❂ ❂ ❂ ❂ ❂ ❂ ❂ ❂ ❂

By the time next summer came around I had pretty much forgotten the hurt I felt last year over wasting my time trying to win one of the bandannas. Money was tight at home and I was lucky to be able to return to camp at all. I resolved to make every minute fun. This would be a summer to remember.

In the morning I bounded out of the cabin in a race to see who would be first at the beach for the daily morning wake-up swim. The third night at camp three of us swiped our counselor's shirt and pants and ran them up the flag pole to be found at the early morning flag raising ceremony. The counselor looked pretty silly saluting the flag in his underwear.

We found the bugler's horn and wadded up a clean hand-kerchief to hide in the end of the horn. The next morning the whole camp got to sleep in an extra five minutes while the bugler tried to figure out why he couldn't blow reveille to wake up the campers. He finally discovered the problem and pulled out the handkerchief. He got even. The following morning he blew the bugle five minutes early. I got a good natured ribbing from the whole camp about that episode.

I headed a delegation of a half-dozen old-time camping buddies to ask that a treasure hunt be initiated as a new pro-ject for the camp. The campers were so enthusiastic about the treasure hunt the staff decided to continue it as a regular activity in later years.

When that mission had been successfully accom-plished, we decided to explore the area on the hilltop next to the camp lodge to dig for Indian artifacts. We believed ancient Indian campgrounds probably had existed on this very spot. That activity was met with great enthusiasm by all 150 campers who were armed with spoons from the dining hall. The search for Indian artifacts came to be known as

"The Great Dig." We actually found some old clay pottery and stone implements that had been left by warriors from an early tribe of Ottawa Indians.

The camp director finally put a stop to the destruction of the yard near the lodge by leading the campers to a more remote area, where we were told Indian arrowheads had been discovered. After digging in the new spot for a couple of days without finding anything we concluded we had been had, but by then we were off on another exciting adventure.

The days went by quickly and I had more fun than ever before. I do not believe I stopped laughing from the beginning of the session until its end. The camp was still awarding the Best Camper awards at the end of the two-week session, but there was not a chance in a blue moon I would win one of the awards. I had more than my share of fun and was always involved in some kind of exciting adventure with other campers. I didn't get anybody in trouble, but I sure had a good time, and so did all my buddies.

The last night of the session we gathered in the lodge for the final powwow. I was in one of the skits presented to the campers for entertainment. When the award ceremony began I was in the back of the room still laughing about some of the evening's hilarity. I knew my name was not going to be called, so I was not paying attention. Suddenly one of my buddies poked me and said, "Hey, Pete, they want you up front."

"Oh, oh," I said. "What have I done now?"

"Go on up front," my buddy said, "you won one of the Best Camper awards."

Sure enough, the camp director handed me one of the twelve beautiful bandannas. I couldn't believe it. I had done nothing to deserve it. I figured I was lucky I didn't get scolded for causing so much commotion in the camp routine. Of course, I had not bothered to make a kerchief band in craft shop this year. There had not been the slightest chance I would win an award for good behavior.

The award ceremony ended and the campers filed out of the assembly room. The camp director was helping one of the staff members put away the stage trappings. I went up to him.

"Mr. Crampton," I said, "can I ask you a question?"

"Sure thing, Pete," he responded. "And by the way, congratulations on winning one of our Best Camper awards."

"I don't understand why I won the award," I said. "Last year I tried like everything to win one of the awards. I guess I must have worked harder than ever, hoping to win one of those bandannas. This year, I decided to forget about it and just had a lot of fun and raised a lot of dickens. I figured I was more in line for some punishment for all of the heck I raised."

The director smiled and extended his hand to shake mine. "Well, I guess you have figured it out, Pete," he said. "The whole point of summer camp is to have good clean fun and help your fellow campers have fun too. I don't think I saw you when you weren't laughing about something or up to some devilment. You livened up things in camp and helped everyone have a good time. You not only had a good time yourself, but you made everyone around you have fun too. You know laughter is contagious. It's good medicine for everyone.

"When the staff voted on who should receive one of the twelve Best Camper awards your name came up first, and you got a unanimous vote in favor from every staff member. In fact," he continued, "we would like to have you back next year as a Junior Counselor, if you are interested."

I was dumfounded, but managed to stammer, "Boy, I sure would." It was the beginning of several wonderful years on staff at YMCA Crystal Lake Camp.

And, I had made a wonderful discovery:

Having fun is good for everyone. If you can make yourself and others around you happy -- that is a healthy way to live your life. No one wants to be around a sourpuss. And no one has much respect for "Mr. Goody-Goody Two Shoes", someone who spends his time trying to impress others. But, spreading a little fun and happiness is a wonderful way to brighten your own life as well as the lives of everyone around you.

Pretty simple formula for a happy life: Have a good time yourself and most of the people around you will have a good time too. Seems like that kinda makes you win twice -- once for yourself and once for your pals, who share the good times with you.

The End

Sweet Sounds of Summer

Is there sweeter music than the
Symphony of children's laughter
Building castles in the sand
At water's edge?

Can the finest singer touch your
Heart as the voice of a sleepy child
Nestled into bed on the porch of
The cottage quietly saying:
> **"Good night Mother."**

What sound conceived can equal the
Robust welcome of a child greeting
His father upon Dad's return from
work at the end of the day with:
> **"Hi, Dad."**

Are there sweeter words to a little
league ball player sliding into home
base than: **"SAFE!"**

Or the shout of Mom and Dad
Over the roar of the crowd.
A victorious shout -- just for you --
When you connect with a fast ball:
      "IT'S A HOME RUN!"

What words of greater triumph than
The cry of a beginning fisherman
Clinging tightly to his fishing pole,
Bobber dipping, pole a-whipping:
      "I GOT HIM! I GOT HIM!"

Is there more soothing summer
Music than cascades of warm rain
Drumming gently on the roof
Of the cottage while leprechauns
Dance around the pot of gold at the
End of the rainbow?

What more hopeful greetings than
Boy to girl, at the beach,
"Hello, my name is Peter."
"Hello, my name is Susan. Where do
You live, Peter?"

Is there a more cheerful voice than
A robin's - cheer, cheer, cheerily
Saying: "Good morning children"?

Or a more spine-tingling call than
The cry of a distant loon echoing
Across the lake?

Is there a friendlier summer sound
Than the crackle of a beach
Campfire piercing the night
While bubbling marshmallows cling
Precariously to a pointed stick?

But best of all,
At the end of a happy summer day
Snuggled safe in Grandma's quilt
The quiet words whispered:
"I love you."

THOSE ARE THE SWEET SOUNDS OF SUMMER

THE ROOSTER WHO CROWED TOO MUCH

Beep, beep! It was the horn on Grandpa's pick up truck. He was returning to the farm from a visit to the County Fair, which was held every year at the end of summer. All the farmers in the county exhibited their finest livestock and the best vegetables at the County Fair.

Grandma came to the door to wave a welcome home to Grandpa as he drove up the driveway. He waved and had a big smile on his face. Grandma could tell Grandpa had been up to something.

"Now what kind of mischief have you been up to?" Grandma asked Grandpa as he walked through the kitchen door.

"Got a great present for you, Mother. Come on out to the truck and I'll show you." He was chuckling to himself and grinning the kind of grin he had when he was up to some kind of devilment.

Grandma shook her head. Most of the time her husband was a level-headed, hard working farmer, but every once in a while he would go off and do something just for the fun of it. She followed Grandpa out to the truck, wondering what it was this time.

Reaching into the truck Grandpa lifted an old blanket that was covering a chicken crate. Inside the crate was a big Rhode Island Red rooster. It stood, blinking its eyes in the sunlight. "Look at that beauty," Grandpa beamed. "That fella ought to make the chickens lay an egg or two. Name is Mr. Kingfish."

"Where in the world did you ever get that rooster?" Grandma asked.

"Found him at the County Fair. He was on sale. Only cost five dollars. Good rooster like that ought to bring twenty dollars."

"What about Percy?" Grandma said. "Percy takes good care of our chickens." Percy was the family's old rooster. He had been in the family for a good number of years. Every chicken farmer needs one rooster, not two. Two roosters on the same farm is one too many.

"This fella will make old Percy toe the mark," Grandpa said. "A little competition never hurt anybody."

"Why was he on sale?" Grandma asked.

"Man said Mr. Kingfish was a little too feisty for his chickens. Gave me a good price. Can't take him back because he was on sale. He'll get along just fine here."

"Well, I don't think it's a very nice thing to do to poor old Percy," Grandma replied. "He has been good to the chickens and we get more eggs than we ever got before Percy. Wakes us up right on time every morning when the sun comes up. Better'n alarm clock."

"Well this is a good lookin' rooster, Mother. See how his tail feathers stick right up and glisten in the sun?"

Just then the rooster threw his head back and let out the loudest cock-a-doodle-doo they had ever heard. Grandma was startled and jumped back.

"Well, I never," she said. "What in the world is he crowing about? It's the middle of the day. Roosters are supposed to crow at the crack of dawn when the sun comes up, not in the middle of the day."

Grandpa laughed. "See, I told you he would wake up things around here. Old Percy never crows during the day."

"Well, I hope he doesn't hurt Percy. Two roosters in the same barnyard can be trouble, you know. They may fight with one another." Grandma turned to walk back in the house while Grandpa opened the chicken crate to let the new rooster loose in the yard. The bird looked around, deciding whether he liked his new home. Then he spied the chickens over by the henhouse. Off he went as fast as his legs could carry him toward the chickens.

Grandpa smiled. This rooster knew what he was here for. He expected the hens would soon start producing twice as many eggs as they did with old Percy in charge.

Then the strangest thing happened. When Mr. Kingfish reached the hens he sat down on the ground and started clucking and squawking. Grandpa could see Mr. Kingfish was a pretty good talker. At first there were a half-dozen hens gathered around. As Mr. Kingfish continued to cluck away, other hens in the barnyard began walking up to him and sat down to listen too. Soon all the chickens in the barnyard had assembled in front of Mr. Kingfish. All of them were listening to the rooster as he clucked an endless stream of chicken words. It looked like he was fascinating the ladies with exciting tales of his travels around the country. It must be admitted, he was a good-looking rooster, with long bronze tail feathers and a bright red wattle hanging below his chin.

Grandpa had never seen anything like it in all his days as a farmer. The hens were gathered around, just sitting on the ground, entranced by Mr. Kingfish's stories. The rooster was a spellbinder all right.

Then suddenly, for no reason at all, Mr. Kingfish stood up, tipped his head back and let out one of the loudest cock-a-doodle-doos Grandpa had ever heard.

Grandma had been watching from the house. She exclaimed, "Why I never. I do believe that rooster is bragging about how important he is! There is no other reason for him to let loose with that kind of racket this time of day. I think we've got ourselves a big blowhard in the barnyard.

"Poor Percy," she sighed. "The new rooster has stolen all his chickens."

Just then Percy peeked his head around the corner of the henhouse. He could see the hens sitting on the ground listening to Mr. Kingfish. Not a single hen was eating or walking around. They were all sitting by Mr. Kingfish as he told them the important things he had done. If they didn't get off the ground pretty soon and start eating the grain Grandma had put out for them there wouldn't be any eggs. Chickens must eat well if they are to lay eggs.

Grandma and Grandpa depended on the eggs to help them make a living. Grandma needed at least two dozen eggs every day to sell at the market in town so the family could have enough money to make ends meet.

Percy called out to the hens, "Stop wasting time listening to that foolishness. Get busy. Our job around here is to lay eggs. If you don't start laying some eggs they'll put all of us in the stew pot for Sunday dinner."

"Oh, go away," one of the chickens called out to Percy. "Can't you see what a splendid rooster he is? He has been everywhere and done everything. He is telling us the most wonderful stories. And he is handsome too."

At that moment Mr. Kingfish saw Percy standing at the corner of the chicken coop. He stood up on his tiptoes, flapped his wings and let out one of his loudest cock-a-doodle-doos. Then, with the meanest look imaginable, Mr. Kingfish put his head down and ran full speed at Percy, with his beak pointed straight ahead like a dangerous spear. It was clear he intended to hurt the older rooster. Not only was Mr. Kingfish a big winded braggart he was a mean bully as well.

Percy jumped to one side, but Mr. Kingfish jabbed him on the leg with his beak. You could tell it hurt. Mr. Kingfish was a lot younger and stronger than Percy. It would not be a fair fight between the two roosters. Percy was smart. He decided it would be best to head for cover. He ducked around the corner.

Mr. Kingfish was very proud of himself. He flapped his wings and jumped on a fence post where he cock-a-doodled for five whole minutes. Some of the younger hens were thrilled with their new hero and enthusiastically clucked their approval. The older hens knew better. Old Percy had taken care of them for a long time. They were not about to abandon their old friend for some young upstart. The older chickens turned and walked away. They would have nothing more to do with the new rooster.

Percy decided it would be best for the time being to find a nice quiet roost in the rafters of the henhouse. This was a problem that required some thinking. Percy flew up into the henhouse rafters, where he quietly settled in to wait it out and to think.

Mr. Kingfish strutted around the farm for a while, pretending he was searching for Percy. He was really just showing off his pretty feathers for the girls. Some of the silly hens thought he was the most magnificent rooster they had ever seen. They watched Mr. Kingfish with fascination, clucking their admiration. Finally, after Mr. Kingfish had paraded as long as possible, he tipped his head back, stood on his tip-toes and let out a triumphant cock-a-doodle-doo.

Then he returned to where he had been telling his stories. The younger ladies gathered around, captivated by his charms. Mr. Kingfish sat down and resumed his stories, telling the girls how he had chased Percy away and other thrilling adventures. Of course, as Mr. Kingfish told it, he was the most glorious hero of all time.

The wiser hens, who knew better, resumed eating the grain Grandma had put out for them. They knew Grandma would be looking for freshly laid eggs first thing in the morning.

The rest of the day Mr. Kingfish continued to recite exciting tales of his past exploits. The listeners were thrilled and sat around all day to hear his stories. The sun finally went down. Not a single egg was laid by the young ladies all day. The older hens did their best to keep up the schedule of producing twenty-four eggs a day, but they could not do everyone's job. The egg production the day Mr. Kingfish arrived was only twelve eggs, half of what it should have been.

At the end of the day, as the sun dipped behind the hills, Mr. Kingfish flew to the roof of the henhouse and let out a mighty cock-a-doodle-doo, once again telling everyone

he was the most important rooster in the whole world. The younger chickens sighed their admiration.

Inside the house Grandma was getting tired of all the rooster's boasting. She had stuffed cotton in her ears to keep out some of the cock-a-doodling. At suppertime, when Grandpa came into the house for his dinner, Grandma said, "Well, Grandpa, your new rooster is making quite a name for himself. He has been holding the silly hens enraptured by his stories most of the day. I don't think we're going to have very many eggs in the morning. The hens have been too busy listening to Mr. Kingfish."

"He has been making quite a racket all right," Grandpa replied. "Don't think I have heard so much crowing by one rooster in a long time. Seems every time I turn around he is a singin' away at the top of his voice. He must be pretty proud of himself."

"Hasn't got anything to be proud of around here," Grandma said. "A lot of those star struck hens haven't done a lick of work or laid a single egg since the bully chased old Percy out of the barnyard. I'm gettin' mighty tired of hearing him brag about himself. Couple more days of this and he'll be headin' for the stew pot."

That night Grandma and Grandpa went to bed. They were tired from all the work they had done during the day. Farm work is very hard and they would have to be up at the crack of dawn the next morning. They settled into bed and were sound asleep by nine o'clock. At midnight they were suddenly awakened by a loud cock-a-doodling. Mr. Kingfish was crowing at the moon.

At one o'clock in the morning Mr. Kingfish awakened everyone again. Then at two Mr. Kingfish decided he should remind everyone how important he was, and he cock-a-doodled until everybody was wide awake again. Every hour after that Mr. Kingfish gave a cock-a-doodle chorus from the top of the henhouse.

By the time Mr. Kingfish announced the rising sun at five o'clock in the morning both Grandma and Grandpa were exhausted. They had hardly slept all night. And none of the chickens had slept either. There would be few eggs laid that day. Chickens and people have to get some rest if they are to do their jobs.

Grandpa was bleary-eyed from lack of sleep. "Well, I guess we know why that darn rooster was on sale. He can't seem to shut his mouth. Never heard such bragging in all my born days."

When Grandma went out to the henhouse to collect the daily supply of eggs she found only twelve eggs. Most of the chickens were wandering around half asleep. Mr. Kingfish had been up most of the night cock-a-doodling. Now he was snoozing in the middle of the henhouse, like he owned it. Grandma picked up a broom and gave him a swat on the behind.

"Okay, Mr. Kingfish, you kept us up all night, now get up yourself." Grandma was real mad. She chased Mr. Kingfish out the door into the barnyard. Mr. Kingfish flew to the top of the henhouse and just sat down, looking at Grandma. He was so full of himself he had no idea why Grandma and some of others didn't adore hearing him brag and cock-a-doodle-doo all the time.

Grandma put the twelve eggs in her basket and walked back into the house. She was cross and irritated. She looked out into the barnyard and saw that Mr. Kingfish had flown down from the roof of the henhouse. Of all the things! There he was once again sitting in the middle of the barnyard talking about himself. Even though the hens were sleepy, Mr. Kingfish held them entranced by his tales. No one could have done all the wonderful things Mr. Kingfish claimed he had, but he was so charming the hens believed every word. They had never seen such a hero -- and here one was, right in their own barnyard. What a thrill.

Soon Mr. Kingfish hopped back up on the fence post and let out one of his cock-a-doodle-doos, loud enough to rouse the whole neighborhood. He continued the racket every hour all day and all night.

The next morning Grandma was about ready to start boiling water for rooster stew. When she went out to the henhouse she only found eight eggs. If the egg production didn't begin to improve soon they might not have enough money to get groceries.

Grandpa had heard all he could stand too. Even though he only paid five dollars for the rooster, he was ready to admit it had been a mistake. Now he knew why Mr. Kingfish was so cheap.

It wouldn't be easy catching him. They could see Mr. Kingfish was smart. All he had to do, if they tried to catch him, was fly to the top of the henhouse. It would be impossible to catch him there.

A moment ago Mr. Kingfish had been sitting on a box at the edge of the barnyard pruning his feathers. The rooster was very proud of his looks and he had just let out one of his loudest cock-a-doodle-doos. Grandpa was drinking a cup of coffee at the kitchen table trying to stay awake. He hadn't had much sleep for the second night in a row.

Grandma looked out the kitchen window. She could see Mr. Kingfish had decided to take a nap. The rooster's eyes were closed. He was still sitting on the box at the edge of the barnyard.

Grandma quietly said to Grandpa, "Take a look, Grandpa. I think our problems may be solved. We may not be able to catch that mean rooster ourselves, but somebody else can. The rooster's been calling too much attention to himself with all the crowing and cock-a-doodling. Here comes Mr. Fox fixin' to get himself a dinner."

Grandpa looked out the window. Sure enough, a red fox was quietly sneaking up on the rooster. They could have yelled a warning to Mr. Kingfish, but they didn't.

Mr. Fox grabbed the obnoxious rooster by his tail feathers and, quick as a wink, yanked him off the box and carried him off across the field.

No one was very sorry to see him go. Even the star struck hens had become tired of listening to Mr. Kingfish repeat the same stories about himself.

And, with the intruder out of the way, Percy came down from his perch in the rafters. It wasn't long before the lady hens started laying eggs again. And everyone enjoyed the quiet.

That was when we realized sometimes there can be too much cock-a-doodle-dooing for a smart rooster's own good.

The End

A Summertime Ballad

Busy day's end on the porch at the cottage
Nestled deep in Gramma's quilt
Hushed by the murmur of still waters
Rinsing the shore close by our resting place.

While far down the lake in hidden bay
The thrill of distant loon calling to the night
Its ancient wilderness ballad
A haunting plea for solitude.

Though we yearn to listen
Sleep cloaks our mind
Within its warm embrace
To dream of pure and noble deeds.

Until the slivers of sunrise
Creep quietly into bed with us
Announcing the morning
With a thousand dancing diamonds upon the lake.

A wondrous start to a fresh born summer day
God's gift to the children of every season.
We gaze in awe at the joyfulness
Of the new day's dawning.

The End

THE STUCK-UP DUCK

The sun was just coming up over the marsh. It was going to be a warm and sunny day, perfect for swimming and splashing around in the lake. Of course to a duck, most every day is nice for swimming and splashing around in the lake, unless the lake was frozen.

Waldo and his duck friends had decided that it would be a good day to swim by the dam at the foot of the lake. They enjoyed going to the dam because they could find lots of good things to eat there. Cattails with delicious roots grew in profusion by the dam, and there was wild celery and rice too. All kinds of things ducks like to eat.

Waldo swam to where his mother was finding food for her twelve new ducklings. He had to wait a minute because his mother was upside down with her tail in the air and her head under water. She was looking for some tender watercress to give to her children. When her head popped up she had a mouthful of watercress. "Hi, Mom," Waldo said. "Some of my pals are going to swim to the dam. They want me to go along. Is it okay if I go with them? We'll be home by suppertime."

Waldo's mother said, "Mpff, wmpf, ffoof, mumf," which meant nothing at all. Her mouth was full of watercress and she couldn't talk.

After Waldo's mother finally swallowed the watercress she replied, "I beg your pardon, Waldo. I couldn't talk. Now what is it you wanted?"

"I'm sorry, Mom. I should have waited until you had a chance to swallow. The guys are going down to the dam and I would like to go along. We promise to be back by suppertime. Can I go, please?"

"Well, promise to stay a good distance away from the dam. Sometimes they let the water out real fast and you could get sucked right through the dam. That happened to Oswald last year. He nearly drowned. Can't be too careful around that dam."

"Gee, thanks, Mom. We'll be careful."

Waldo swam out to the middle of the lake to join his friends who were waiting for him. They splashed water on each other and happily began swimming down the lake toward the dam.

For a duck, going to the dam where there is wild rice, celery and cattail roots is like going to the candy store, except they don't need any money. It's all free to ducks.

As the ducks swam down the lake they passed close by an island. The island had tall reeds growing in the water along its shore. Waldo had seen a family of very large ducks who had a nest among the reeds. Waldo and his friends had never played with the kids in that family. All of them looked like they were very stuck-up. They swam around all day with their noses high in the air. Nobody likes a duck who is snooty. That's what they call ducks who go around with their noses stuck up -- snooty.

As Waldo and his pals passed close by the island they could see two of the stuck-up ducks swimming among the reeds. The stuck-up ducks looked at Waldo and his friends, but they did not say hello. That was okay with Waldo. Who likes to play with snooty ducks anyway?

Soon Waldo and his friends were close to the dam. Waldo called out to his buddies, "Stay away from the dam, fellas. It's dangerous if they decide to let the water out."

"Yeah, sure, scaredy cat," one of the ducks replied. "That's where the best celery grows. We'll get the good stuff. You just look out for yourself."

Waldo knew the best wild celery grew right next to the dam because none of the older ducks took the chance of getting sucked into the dam. They left the wild celery close to the dam alone. It was too risky.

No use arguing with some of his smart-alecky buddies. Waldo headed for the shore, well away from the dam. There was plenty of wild rice and cattail roots without getting too close to the dam. Waldo would have lunch by himself.

As Waldo swam along the shore looking for a good place to have lunch he had his head under water. When he came up for a breath of air there was one of the big stuck-up ducks swimming right alongside.

"Hello," the stuck-up duck said.

"Well, hello," Waldo replied. "Are you from the island we just passed?"

"Yes, that's where we live with my mother and dad. We have a nest on the edge of the island among the reeds. My mother is sitting on her eggs right now. I expect we'll have some brothers and sisters soon."

"That's nice," Waldo said. "I have twelve new brothers and sisters myself. They're not old enough to come to the dam. They have to stay with Mom. I came down the lake with some of my friends to have some lunch. Do you like wild celery?"

"Oh sure," the stuck-up duck replied. "But tell your friends not to get too close to the dam. If they decide to let the water out your buddies could get sucked right into the dam. They could drown. The current gets very strong when they open the gates. It's dangerous."

"I warned the guys," Waldo said, "but they paid no attention."

"Well, let's hope they don't get too close," the stuck-up duck said as he turned to swim away. "Nice meeting you," he called out to Waldo as he swam away. "Stop by some time."

Waldo waved and turned to look for some wild celery. He thought the stuck-up duck wasn't such a bad guy after all. He seemed friendly enough, even if his nose was way up in the air like a snooty duck's.

Suddenly Waldo heard one of his friends down by the dam hollering. "Get back! Get back! They are letting water out of the dam. The current will drag you under!"

Waldo looked toward the dam. One of his friends was swimming as fast as he could away from the dam. Two more of Waldo's friends were floundering in the water close to the dam. The current was dragging them under. Waldo frantically started swimming toward the dam. He could feel the strong current pulling him toward the dam. If he got much closer, it

would drag him under too and he could drown along with his two friends.

Waldo's two friends still had their heads above water. They were paddling as hard as they could against the fast current, but they were tiring rapidly. It wouldn't be much longer and they could be goners. Waldo didn't know what to do. If he got any closer he could be sucked under too. If the force of the current pinned them against the dam all three would drown. Even though ducks can hold their breath under water for a long time they have to come up for air eventually.

Waldo knew there was no time to lose. He had to act quickly or it would be too late. He decided he had to help his friends, even at the risk of his life. He began paddling toward the dam as fast as he could.

As he got closer he could feel the strong undertow dragging him toward the dam.

Just then the stuck-up duck Waldo had been talking to a minute earlier went racing past. As the stuck-up duck charged full speed toward the dam he yelled to Waldo, "Stay back. Stay back. I'll get them."

Waldo stopped just in time. He could barely hold his own against the rushing current. He turned around and, with a burst of energy, managed to swim away from the dam until he reached still water, where he could no longer feel the pull of the current. Then he watched helplessly as the stuck-up duck raced toward Waldo's two friends. Only their noses were above water. They could not fight the undertow much longer.

The stuck-up duck reached Waldo's friends just as they were going under. He grabbed both of them by a foot and turned back, pulling the two ducks away from the dam with strong kicks of his feet.

It was a desperate struggle, but they made it. Waldo's friends came up gasping and fighting for a breath of air. The stuck-up duck was exhausted too. Free from the pull of the current they all swam to shore where they could rest.

Waldo looked at the stuck-up duck who had flopped down on the shore, trying to catch his breath. It was obvious he had nearly been done in by the struggle.

"Gee, thanks," Waldo said. "My friends would have surely drowned if you had not come to their rescue. Me too, if I had gotten any closer to the dam. You saved all of our lives. You are very brave and strong to have risked your life to save us. You don't even know us.

"We swim past your island every day, but we never stopped to say hello," Waldo said. "We just guessed you wouldn't want to talk to us. We thought you were stuck-up. Your nose is pretty high up you know. Kind of snooty."

The stuck-up duck had caught his breath by now. He laughed.

"Well, I'm real glad we finally had a chance to meet," the stuck-up duck said. "I have been wishing you and your pals would invite me to join you when you go swimming in the lake. I would have asked if I could play with you, but you always seemed to avoid me.

"I'm afraid you've got me all wrong. I'm not snooty or stuck-up at all. It's true my nose is pretty high up. But it's not because I am stuck-up. It's because I'm a goose."

The End

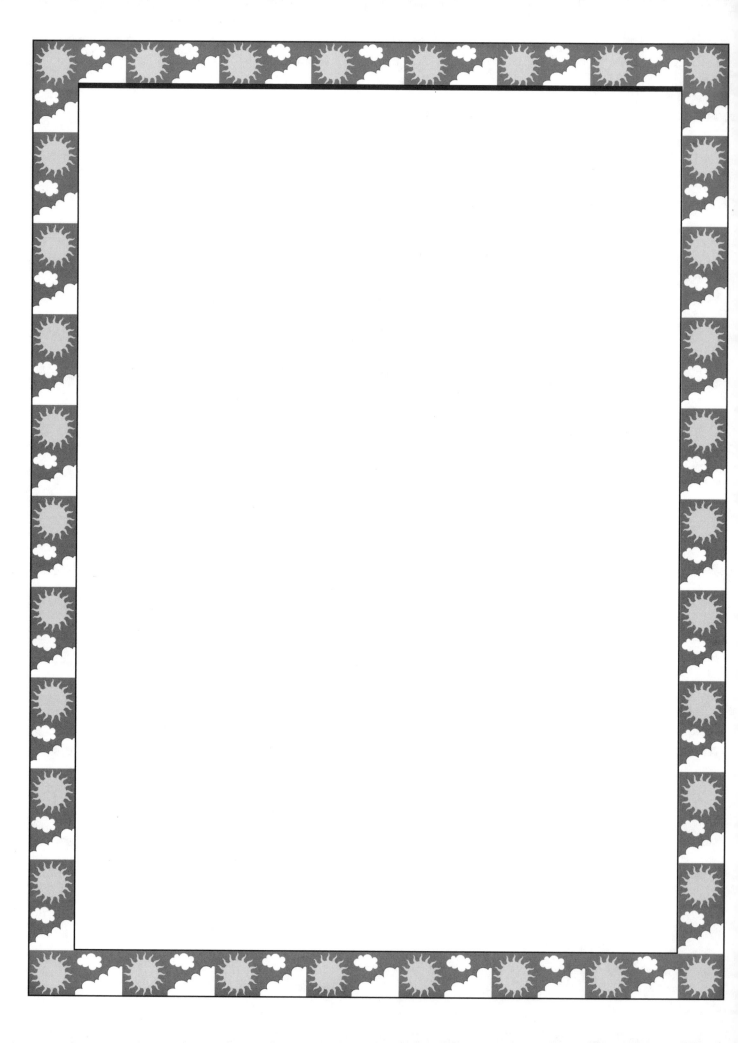

BABYSITTING WITH AUNT RACHAEL

Aunt Rachael had stopped over to have dinner with her sister's family.

"You sure it's all right, Rachael?" her sister asked following dinner.

"Of course," Aunt Rachael replied. "You two don't get a chance to go out often. I have nothing to do. I'll be delighted to look after the kids while you go to the movies."

Aunt Rachael had volunteered to babysit her two nieces while her sister and her brother-in-law went to a special movie they wanted to see. Aunt Rachael had no children of her own. She adored her two nieces, Leslie, age four, and Elizabeth, age six.

"Well," Aunt Rachael's sister said, "we do want to see that movie. If you're sure it won't be a bother we'd appreciate you looking after the kids. They can keep busy reading the new books Elizabeth received on her birthday last week. The children should be in bed by eight. We'll be home by nine-thirty."

"That's fine," Aunt Rachael replied. "We'll have a good time, won't we girls?"

"Can we play some games, Aunt Rachael?" Leslie asked. Leslie loved any kind of game and she loved her Aunt Rachael even more.

"Sure we can," Aunt Rachael said. "Let's read one of Elizabeth's new birthday books and then we can play our fun game."

"Hide-and-seek!" both children cried at once.

"That's the one," Aunt Rachael said.

The children lived in a big house. The house was at least a hundred years old and had many nooks and crannies, closets and secret hiding places. The children loved hiding from their aunt. Aunt Rachael could always find them because they couldn't stop giggling. Their giggles gave them away.

"Okay," the children's mother said. "Have a good time and into bed by eight o'clock." Then, turning to Aunt Rachael, she said, "Don't let them talk you into staying up later than eight. Sometimes they can talk you into most anything, you know. They'll try to get you to let them stay up."

"Don't worry", Aunt Rachael replied. "They'll be tucked in by eight, I promise." She smiled at the children, giving them a big wink of her eye. "It'll be the cat-o'-nine-tails for anyone still up when the clock strikes eight. Right, guys?"

The children giggled. They knew their aunt well. She could no more punish them than the man in the moon.

As the parents went out the door Aunt Rachael called after them, "Have a good time and don't worry. I'll put them to bed by eight."

As the car drove away, Aunt Rachael addressed the children. "Okay, girls, first we have to clear the table and do the dishes. Then we'll decide on a book to read. When we finish the book we can play hide-and-seek."

After the dinner dishes had been washed and put away the children decided they wanted Aunt Rachael to read to them *Little Red Riding Hood,* one of the books Elizabeth had received for her birthday.

The children snuggled next to Aunt Rachael on the living room couch as they read the book together. At the end of the story, Leslie asked, "Now can we play hide-and-seek, Aunt Rachael?"

"Okay," Aunt Rachael replied. "But remember. The last time we played I found you when you gave yourselves away by giggling. You would have won if you hadn't started laughing. This time, remember, no giggling."

The children giggled. "We go first, Aunt Rachael."

"Five minutes, and here I come," said Aunt Rachael, as the children scurried from the room.

She waited until all was quiet in the big house and then announced, "Time's up. Here I come, ready or not."

It was fun playing hide-and-seek with Aunt Rachael. She always warned of her approach with things like, "Here comes the giant, looking for little children to eat. The giant loves to eat children for dessert." Sometimes she would call out, "No giggling now. The giant has big ears and can hear children giggling." That would almost always make the girls begin to laugh, giving themselves away.

Aunt Rachael soon found Leslie hidden under the kitchen sink. Then both of them searched for Elizabeth. They found her under the bed in her parent's bedroom.

"Okay," the children said, "your turn Aunt Rachael. Go hide. We'll find you."

Aunt Rachael made them close their eyes and then very quietly she slipped into the front hall closet, right next to where the children were sitting in the dining room. It would be easy for the children to find her.

But it was too easy. The children thought their aunt would hide in a better place than the front hall closet. They began roaming the house searching in every secret place. They searched for more than a half hour, but no Aunt Rachael. At first Aunt Rachael had been standing up behind the coats hanging in the closet. She waited, but no one found her. She decided to sit down on the floor of the closet.

After a while the children got tired of searching. They forgot all about hide-and-seek and returned to the dining room where Elizabeth kept her new birthday presents. They began playing with Elizabeth's new games.

Aunt Rachael could hear the children in the dining room, which was only a few steps from where she was hiding. At first she thought they were still looking for her. Finally she realized they had given up looking. She was tired of

COUGH!

waiting to be found in the closet, so she decided a quiet cough might help the girls find her. She coughed. The children paid no attention. They heard their aunt cough and knew where she was hiding, but their games were more fun.

Elizabeth put her finger in front of her lips and whispered to Leslie, "Let's pretend we don't know where she is hiding." They decided to let their aunt stay hidden in the closet.

Sitting in the quiet of the closet all by herself, Aunt Rachael began to get drowsy. Soon she was fast asleep, sitting on the closet floor.

At eight o'clock the children put away their games and peeked in the closet where they knew Aunt Rachael was hiding. They found her, sitting on the floor, sound asleep. They put a blanket over their aunt to keep her warm, softly closed the closet door and, without being told, crept quietly upstairs to bed.

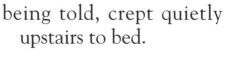

The children brushed their teeth and put on their pajamas. They climbed into their beds. The sandman sprinkled his magic dust and sleep came quickly to the

children. All the while, Aunt Rachael was sound asleep herself, on the floor of the front hall closet.

At nine-thirty the children's parents returned from the movies. The house was quiet. They opened the closet door to hang up their coats and there was Aunt Rachael, fast asleep, covered with a blanket on the closet floor.

"What in the world, Rachael? What are you doing in the closet?" her sister exclaimed.

Roused from her slumber, Aunt Rachael blinked her eyes. "I'm waiting for the children to find me," she said. "We're playing hide-and-seek. It's my turn to hide."

The girls' father came downstairs from checking on the children. "The children are fine," he said. "They are sound asleep in their beds."

"Yes," said Aunt Rachael. "I told them they would have to be in bed by eight o'clock.

"Well, I better run along," she said, as she folded the blanket and handed it to her sister. "I hope you enjoyed the movie."

Aunt Rachael put on her coat, said good-bye, and walked out the front door to return to her home. As she climbed into her car, she said to herself, "I'll bet those little rascals knew where I was hiding all along. They put themselves to bed all by themselves. Sometimes I think they are more grown-up than I am.

"I wonder, who was the babysitter -- me -- or the children?"

The End

A WALK IN THE WOODS WITH GRANDMA

"Grandma," Martha said, "can we take a walk in the woods this afternoon?" It was a beautiful, warm, spring day. Martha was visiting her grandmother on the farm for the weekend.

"That would be nice," Martha's grandmother replied, "but first you have to give me time to finish making this apple pie. Want to help?"

"Oh, yes, can I help cut the apples?" Martha asked. She loved helping her grandmother in the kitchen. Grandma always made Martha feel welcome in her kitchen, even though Martha knew sometimes she was more of a bother than a help.

"Be careful with the sharp knife," Grandmother replied, handing Martha a paring knife. "Peel off the skin of the apple and try to leave as much of the apple as you can."

That was one thing Martha liked about helping her grandmother. If Martha peeled the skin of the apples too thick, taking too much of the inside of the apple along with the peel, her grandmother never bawled her out. They just laughed about it together.

Her grandmother always made fun. She would say things like, "Well, Martha, looks like your grandpa isn't going to get much pie for dessert tonight. We just cut off his share of the pie along with the apple peel. If he wants more pie we'll just let him do his own peeling."

Martha knew her grandmother was only fooling. It was Grandma's way of telling Martha to be more careful how she peeled the apples without hurting Martha's feelings or discouraging Martha from helping in the kitchen. When Grandma said something like that they would both giggle; most often followed by a hug from Grandma. Grandma was the best teacher ever.

"When we go for our walk this afternoon," Grandma said, "promise me you'll let me walk real slow. I can't keep up with you young folks, you know."

Grandma was plenty spry. She could walk the legs off you if she wanted. But that wasn't the way she liked to walk when they went for a walk in the woods. Going for a walk with Grandma was more like exploring.

After lunch the two of them put on light sweaters. Even though it was a warm spring day the woods would still be cool. Grandma put on her walking shoes. They headed out the back door, down the lane to the woods. As they walked along, hand in hand, Grandma said, "Now we must be real quiet. Right along here is where the killdeer has built its nest. Maybe she will put on a show for us."

Suddenly a large bird, twice as big as a robin, flew from its nest on the ground ahead of them. It had long slender wings, a grayish-brown back and a light-colored breast marked with black bands. Instead of flying away the bird landed only a short distance out in the field; fluttering to the ground as if it couldn't fly. Martha and her grandmother stopped walking and watched. The bird ran along the ground out into the field dragging one wing behind it.

"Oh, Grandma," Martha said, "it's hurt. It can't fly."

"Don't worry Martha," her Grandmother quietly replied, "it's a killdeer and it's just pretending."

"Why is it pretending, Grandma?"

"It wants us to follow it out into the field, away from its nest. The nest is up ahead, alongside the edge of the field. If we keep walking the bird will come back to its nest. If it is away from the nest too long the eggs will cool off and they won't hatch."

Martha and her grandmother continued walking, but out of the corner of their eyes they watched as the killdeer fluttered about in the field making a big commotion and dragging one wing as if it had been broken. As soon as Martha and her grandmother had walked past the nest the bird flew into the air and returned to sit on its eggs.

"Look, Grandma, the bird's wing is all better!" Martha exclaimed.

"She was just pretending all along," Grandma said with a chuckle. "That's the way they hide their nests. They think we might try to take the eggs, so they run along the ground pretending to be injured. If a fox came along it he would be tempted to follow the bird, thinking the bird couldn't fly and hoping to catch an easy meal. The bird would just keep moving further and further away from the nest, staying out of reach until the fox forgot where the bird flew up. Foxes don't often catch killdeer or bother their nests. Killdeer are too smart for a fox."

As Martha and her grandmother neared the edge of the woods an animal a little bigger than a large squirrel waddled out into the open field. It's color was light gray, almost white. It had a long, skinny tail. "Why there's Mister Possum," Grandma said. "He likes to play tricks too, just like the killdeer. Run out there acting like you want to catch him, but don't get too close. They have sharp teeth."

Martha ran out into the field after the possum. A possum can't run very fast. Suddenly the animal lay down on the ground and curled up in a ball. Martha remembered her grandmother's warning and didn't get any closer. As she watched, the possum pretended to be sound asleep. She could see the possum's eyes were closed and it lay completely still, so still it looked as if it had simply died of fright. But it was only pretending, just like the killdeer.

"That's how a possum protects itself," Grandma said. "Many animals have no interest in another animal they think is dead. Mr. Possum pretends he is dead so a predator will go away and leave him alone. It's a trick they have. We call it 'playing possum'. As soon as we move along he will get up and climb a tree. Usually they live up in the trees for protection. But they can be mean animals if they are cornered. Best to leave Mr. Possum alone."

As Martha and her grandmother entered the woods they could feel the cool shelter of the canopy of new spring leaves. There was not a sound. It was as if all the birds and animals had gone away. But they were there. The birds had stopped singing and the animals were hiding, watching the invaders to see if they posed any danger.

Grandma found a large fallen tree just right for a place to sit. She sat down without a word and Martha sat alongside her. It was very quiet.

Gradually, one by one, as Martha and her grandmother sat quietly not saying a word, the birds began flitting about among the tree branches. First one sang and then another. It was not long before the forest was filled with the songs of happy birds calling to each other.

"What do you suppose they are saying?" Martha's grandmother whispered.

"Are they saying hello to us, Grandma?" Martha quietly replied.

"I believe some of them may be telling the other birds we seem friendly and not to be afraid. The bolder ones may be saying hello, welcoming us into the forest. It is their home you know. We have to let them know we are their friends."

"How do we let them know we are their friends?" Martha whispered.

"By sitting still and not making any noise. Pretty soon they'll decide they have nothing to fear from us."

There were other animals in the woods watching them too. One was a black squirrel, peeking at them from the top of a large oak tree. As Martha and her grandmother remained very quiet the squirrel decided he would investigate. They spied the squirrel when he crept along the top of a large branch to peer down at them. When they seemed not to notice, he swished his tail, deliberately trying to get their attention. Martha and her grandmother watched without a word. Squirrels are naturally curious and it was not long before he began to slowly steal down the other side of the tree, peeking out from time to time, all the while keeping a wary eye on Martha and her grandmother.

Finally, the squirrel decided they intended no harm. He jumped the last few feet to the ground and began digging among the fallen leaves on the forest floor looking for the acorns he had hidden last fall. The squirrel pretended Martha and her grandmother weren't there and Martha and her grandmother pretended they didn't see the squirrel. There was a lot of pretending going on.

As Martha and her grandmother sat quietly Martha thought she saw movement out the corner of her eye. She slowly turned her head. There was a white-tailed deer followed closely by her spotted fawn. The fawn could only be a day or two old for it was still unsteady on its feet.

The deer had not seen the visitors and continued walking toward Martha and her grandmother. The mother deer paused every once in a while to scrape the ground with its front hoofs looking for a fallen acorn to eat. Martha had seen grownup deer before, but she had never seen a newborn fawn. It was exciting. She sat perfectly still, pressing her lips tightly closed so that she would not make a sound.

The big deer continued rummaging through the leaves under the oak tree searching for acorns. It paid no attention to the squirrel who was also digging through the leaves seeking something to eat. As the deer gradually circled the big oak tree the mother deer suddenly lifted her head to sniff the air. A gentle breeze had carried the smell of the intruders to the deer's nose. The doe spied Martha and her grandmother sitting quietly on the log. It stamped the earth, alerting the fawn to danger and snorted a warning. Then it wheeled about, threw its tail into the air and bounded away.

At first the fawn didn't know what to make of the commotion. It had never seen people before and saw no reason to be afraid. But it knew for sure it had better follow its

mother. As if propelled by a large spring, the little fawn leaped into the air, turned and ran after its mother as fast as its new legs could manage.

As the two deer disappeared into the woods, Grandma said, "That was exciting, wasn't it, Martha?"

"Oh, yes," Martha replied. "I have never seen a baby deer before."

They decided to continue their walk in the woods. They began walking slowly along a path through the woods. But they never got more than a few steps at a time. It seemed that Grandma had to stop at every new variety of wildflower or mushroom to examine it. She never picked the flowers or pulled them up. She knelt down beside every plant, tenderly lifting the blossoms to admire each tiny feature.

The forest was filled with beautiful white Trillium blossoms. "Look, Martha," Grandma said, "see how the whole forest seems to come alive, as if lighted by the glow of a thousand white candles? A special birthday party to celebrate the coming of spring.

"And look at these Wild Violets adding frosting to the birthday cake. Aren't they the most beautiful shades of pink and yellow you ever did see?"

As they continued slowly through the woods, Martha watched her grandmother tenderly admiring each new plant, as if discovering its beauty for the first time. Martha began to understand how much her grandmother appreciated and loved the delicate beauty of the forest.

And it wasn't long before Martha too began to appreciate the loveliness contained within Mother Nature's tiniest creations -- often the smallest had the most intricate beauty of all -- if you took the time to look ever so closely.

"I do believe I love the Spring Beauties more than any other," Grandma said, gazing at a clump of small wild plants on the forest floor. "We are lucky to find them. They only last a few days at the beginning of spring." The Spring Beauties, as they were named, had tiny pink flowers shaped like five-pointed stars, each petal perfectly formed.

"Oh, Grandma!" Martha exclaimed as they came to an opening in the forest carpeted with white and lavender blossoms.

"We have discovered the secret hiding place of the Hepaticas, Martha. Hepaticas are one of the first wildflowers to come up each spring."

The beautiful small flowers had six light-purple petals with a tiny bouquet of delicate golden fingers radiating from their center. The small plants, interspersed among last year's fallen twigs and crumpled leaves, lighted by bits and pieces of sunbeams filtering through the trees, seemed to give the woods a happy smile.

"And look," Grandma exclaimed, "here is a Lady's Slipper just beginning to bloom." A single stem stretched up from large green leaves at the base of the plant. The long stem was capped by a most unusual orange-colored blossom, resembling the wings and body of a giant honey bee.

Grandma could not be hurried. She found beauty in every plant -- in every living thing.

"Come see the Indian's war paint plant," Grandma said as she knelt beside a plant bearing a large white flower. The plant had lush green leaves and a thick orange root. "This is a Bloodroot Plant. The Indians painted themselves with the red sap from the plant's root. The warriors looked most ferocious with red-painted faces. The red masks they painted on their faces were intended to strike fear into the hearts of their enemies, scaring them away. It worked too. That was much better than having to fight and risk their lives."

As the two explorers continued their journey through the forest they saw a pond ahead. "We must be real quiet here," Grandma whispered. "All kinds of creatures live in the pond. We don't want them to be frightened." They could hear the voices of the frogs as they drew nearer.

They crept through the woods to the edge of the pond, sitting down on a large gnarled root that had grown out of the ground from a very old cedar tree. They had not disturbed the frogs who continued their boisterous chorus.

"HAR-UMPH, HAR-UMPH," -- the frogs called out. First from one end of the pond and then from the other end of the pond. **"HAR-UMPH, HAR-UMPH."** Each bullfrog was trying to sing louder than his competitor at the opposite end of the pond.

"What are they saying, Grandma?" Martha whispered.

"Those are bullfrogs and they are probably saying:

'Here I am, ladies. I'm the biggest old bullfrog in this whole pond. Come on over here and pay a visit. We'll have the nicest bunch of young tadpoles you ever did see.' "

"Is that really what they are saying, Grandma?"

Martha's grandmother chuckled and hugged her granddaughter, "Well, I don't know for sure what they are saying because I've never been a bullfrog myself. But that's probably what they are saying. That's what most bullfrogs say most of the time. Especially in the spring. Springtime is when they're proudest and loudest."

Then Grandma added with a smile, "Boys are like that, you know."

Martha giggled.

They sat by the pond for a long time, neither saying a word. The sun was out and it was warm and pleasant. They just soaked up the quiet joy of living that seems to come with the woods. It's a spirit that is always in the forest, but you have to sit very quietly for a long time or you'll miss it. Lots of people never sit still long enough to feel it. They miss a lot of joy and peace in their lives.

It wasn't long before a large duck emerged from the rushes on the other side of the pond. The duck had a shiny green head and green feathers at its wing tips. "That's the daddy," Grandma whispered.

Martha watched, but did not say a word. Soon the mother duck stuck her head out from the rushes. Finding no danger, she followed the papa duck out into the pond leading a string of seven yellow ducklings. The ducklings skittered here and there on the surface of the pond, playing and racing with each other, but they never went very far away from their mother.

Martha and her grandmother watched the games the small baby ducks played while their mother searched for tender roots in the bottom of the pond. Finally the duck family disappeared behind a patch of rushes at the other end of the pond. They had never been the least bothered by Martha and her grandmother sitting alongside the pond.

It was time to return home. They stood up and began to retrace their steps back toward the farm. While they were walking the birds continued to sing. They saw the black squirrel still searching for acorns. None of the animals were disturbed by their presence. They even caught a glimpse of the deer watching them from the edge of the woods as they strolled along the path. The birds and animals were no longer afraid of the visitors.

By being friendly to the forest and to the birds and animals and flowers Martha and her grandmother were no longer intruders. They had become a part of the forest itself. They could come for a visit any time.

Martha decided it was a good feeling to know they belonged.

The End

Summer's End

The days grow short, the mornings crisp.
The signs of fall are here.
Time for summer's sad farewell.
This bittersweet time of year.

Our lazy days of fun and play
Now must end. That's the rule.
Time to get our books and pens.
Time for our return to school.

Winter nods its frosty greeting.
Children's happy cries are hushed.
Now we gather up the toys.
An end to summer's busy rush.

Soon snow will fall, cold and harsh.
Time to find that misplaced mitten.
Back to school to read our books.
There to learn what has been written.

As if to soothe this anxious time.
Nature gives its autumn show.
Brilliant reds midst amber's blaze.
A magic time with golden glow.

Each keen breeze rains crumpled leaves.
Tumbling to the forest floor.
Lone crimson leaf flutters in the wind.
Directing autumn's triumphal score.

Though summer sun has faded.
Bright rays of season past.
We have our fondest memories.
Happy times will always last.

Warm thoughts of distant summer friends
Bring smiles to our lips, words we still hear.
A misty time for misty eyes.
This bittersweet time of year.